"I DON'T THINK A MAN'S EVER COOKED FOR ME BE-fore," Ellen said.

"I'm the first?" Jonah asked.

"You're the first."

"Well, I don't know if throwing slabs of meat on the barbecue is really cooking," he said, looking up from slicing and dicing the salad ingredients. "But I'm trying to impress you here, so we'll go with that." He motioned to the counter in front of him. "And the mangling of vegetables, of course."

There was no mistaking his eagerness to dazzle her. The table set for two with candles and flowers, his frequent glances at the level of wine in her glass, and his constant awareness of her position in the room were heartbreakingly sweet.

She took a sudden left turn. "Jonah," she said impulsively.

"Yes." He stopped what he was doing to answer her.

With two and a half steps and all the courage she could muster, she wedged herself between him and the counter. "I'm already impressed."

No words could describe the subtle change in his expression that spoke directly to her heart, that seemed to welcome her home and promise an exciting adventure all at once. His gaze roamed slowly over her hair to her lips, across her cheeks and chin, deep into her eyes, and inside her soul, claiming it all as his own.

"So am I. . . ."

WHAT ARE *LOVESWEPT* ROMANCES?

They are stories of true romance and touching emotion. We believe those two very important ingredients are constants in our highly sensual and very believable stories in the LOVE-SWEPT line. Our goal is to give you, the reader, stories of consistently high quality that may sometimes make you laugh, sometimes make you cry, but are always fresh and creative and contain many delightful surprises within their pages.

Most romance fans read an enormous number of books. Those they truly love, they keep. Others may be traded with friends and soon forgotten. We hope that each LOVESWEPT romance will be a treasure—a "keeper." We will always try to publish

LOVE STORIES YOU'LL NEVER FORGET
BY AUTHORS YOU'LL ALWAYS REMEMBER

The Editors

Loveswept ® 915

BY THE
BOOK

MARY KAY
McCOMAS

BANTAM BOOKS
NEW YORK · TORONTO · LONDON · SYDNEY · AUCKLAND

BY THE BOOK
A Bantam Book / December 1998

ISBN 0-553-44624-X

Published simultaneously in the United States and Canada

PRINTED IN THE UNITED STATES OF AMERICA

OPM   10 9 8 7 6 5 4 3 2 1

To everyone who ever worked at
Bantam Loveswept,
thank you

CHAPTER ONE

STEP ONE

In the long run, we hit only what we aim at.
—Henry David Thoreau

Henry had a point. A good one. Determine exactly what it is you want. You can't have your way unless you know which way you want to go. Be practical. Be realistic. Reach for the stars . . . but stay in your own galaxy.

Waiting for a blue, two-tone station wagon to back out of a parking space in the crowded lot at the supermarket, Ellen Webster looked up in time to see a woman in a green Volkswagen swing around the corner just as the elderly couple pulled away, and drive straight into the open space. . . .

A short time later, while waiting at the deli counter, she watched a small child topple a display of boxed crackers. She stepped forward to help the harried mother set the disarray right. When she set the last box in place, she turned to see she'd not only lost her place in line, but the mother and child were walking away with enough thin-sliced bologna to plug a pothole in a country road. . . .

A portly, out-of-breath man with thick glasses and a cane bumped into her shopping cart with his at the checkout counter.

"Oh. Excuse me," he said, squinting to see her.

"No problem," she said, backing up a bit to let him go first.

"I think you were here before me." He was wheezing heavily, as he swung an arm wide to usher her through.

"That's okay," she said, noting his pallor and the thin layer of perspiration on his brow and upper lip. "You don't have much there. Go ahead of me."

"Thank you." He pushed his cart into the narrow aisle as the person in front of them paid her bill and gathered up her groceries.

The man fished around in his cart and picked up the first thing he touched, a head of rusty iceberg lettuce, and set it on the moving belt. She frowned. Poor guy. Can't see well enough to get a good head of lettuce, she thought, watching it travel toward the cashier.

That was when the sirens began to blare and the store lights started to flash off and on. Beethoven's Ninth Symphony came blasting over the loudspeakers.

"What? What?" the man cried out in confusion, raising his cane in the air, swinging it back and forth.

"Congratulations, sir," she heard the teller tell him as she ducked the cane. "It's Lowry's tenth anniversary and you're our one hundredth customer today. You've just won five hundred dollars, sir!"

"Well, fancy that," he said.

Fancy that indeed. She released a sigh of abdication that she'd been holding in her lungs for half her lifetime. She closed her eyes and bent her head, wagging it slowly.

It wasn't that she hated her life. She didn't. For the most part, it was self-designed and tailored to fit her perfectly. Still, there was this unshakable suspicion that something was terribly wrong with it.

If the meek were to inherit the earth, she wasn't getting her share. Doing unto others as you would have them do unto you was simply another dogmatic dud, if you asked her.

Good guys always finish last was an adage that better depicted her life.

Only the good die young was an expression that was beginning to make absolute sense to her.

What was she doing wrong? she wondered, not for the first time, as she opened her eyes to see the fat, blear-eyed man waving five crisp one-hundred-dollar bills in her face.

She smiled weakly at him, knowing he wouldn't be able to decipher her insincerity. *Let a smile be your umbrella,* people said. All she ever got was a mouthful of rain.

She backed away from the checkout stand, where the manager was shaking the winner's hand and posing for pictures, and moved three aisles down to a line that was still moving.

Politely encouraging other people to take the winner's position in front of her was becoming a terrifying and familiar experience. Just that morning she'd accidentally discovered that the young girl she'd trained as a teller at the bank was not only making fifty cents more an hour than she was, but was also being considered for the temporary loan officer's job that would be opening up when Mary Westford went on maternity leave.

Last month her sister, Jane, had complained that she was tired of the same old summer resort she and her family had been vacationing at for the past few years. Ellen merely mentioned how much she'd enjoyed the quiet little seaside town of Rainbow Beach the summer before. There wasn't a room to be had when she'd called around the village four days earlier, and yet somehow her sister had managed to find a condo for three whole weeks.

She stepped to the front of her shopping cart to unload her groceries onto the rolling black belt. Apples. Onions. Gourmet cat food. Breakfast cereal. Shampoo. Gourmet cat food. Paper towels . . .

And then there was the mystery man. She sighed. So attractive. And he had that big flashy smile that he aimed at everyone but her. He'd reopened the camera shop across the street from the bank about a month ago. His shoulders were very broad. He'd been out washing his front display window that morning when the bank opened. She could see him from her cubicle in Bonds and Trusts. The muscles in his arms had strained and corded under his T-shirt when he'd reached to get the high spots; his short wavy brown hair had been streaked with gold in the morning sun.

Why hadn't she kept her mouth shut about him?

"Where are you this morning?" she'd heard her friend Violet ask as she sat with her chin on her fist watching him. "I've answered your line twice already."

"My line?" she'd asked, looking at her phone to see three lights blinking on hold. "Oh. Sorry." She'd looked at Vi and laughed at herself. "Well, it's clear I'm not really here yet, isn't it?"

Vi had leaned against the wall of the small cubicle while Ellen answered and quickly dispatched her calls.

"He's a nice distraction, isn't he?" Vi had asked, thoughtfully twisting a long curl of her blond hair around her finger. "Have you noticed how often he washes that front window?"

"Who?"

"That beautiful hunk-o-man across the street," Vi had said with a knowing smile and a sly glance toward the front window. "Your view is better than mine, by the way."

"Does that mean you're going to be standing there all day?"

"Nah. I got work to do. I'll leave as soon as he bends over to pick up all those paper towels on the sidewalk."

Ellen couldn't help herself. She had looked. Just in time to watch him bend over and pick up the dirty paper towels, displaying for the entire world behind him a rather nice picture of the seat of his pants.

"Okay. My day is made," Vi had said, pushing away from the wall with a satisfied grin on her face. Then she'd grown thoughtful. "I wonder how much a good camera would cost? And how long it would take me to figure out how it works? And which film to use? And then there's always all those lenses to get into. . . ."

"Go for it," she'd said, understanding her perfectly. Blindly shuffling papers across her desk, she knew full well that Vi had a better chance of attracting the man's attention than she did . . . and wished it weren't true. "Your handle has room for one more notch on it."

Vi had laughed. "That's why I carry the big guns, baby. Plenty of space for my notches."

She'd nodded, agreeing, trying to look busy and un-interested in Vi's social life—which consisted primarily of discovering what a man would fall for, rather than what he stood for. Her idea of a truly romantic setting was something with a diamond or a sapphire in it.

"They say," Vi had said enticingly, "he used to work for the CIA."

"I heard it was the FBI."

Vi had laughed. "I heard he was a spy. But before I heard that, I heard he was some kind of war hero turned mercenary. I heard he's some sort of relative to old man Blake who's come here to help him out till he's back on his feet."

"I heard long-lost son," Ellen had said experimentally.

"I heard nephew."

They'd stared at each other for a second, then laughed. How could she not like Vi? She simply *was* the sort of person Ellen wished she could be. Bold and sassy.

"Maybe we should mosey on over and check out his inventory during lunch," Vi had suggested. "Start up a conversation. Find out what's what."

"Can't. Not today. Promised Mrs. Phipps I'd pick up a few things for her at the grocery store. You go on without me. Take notes."

"You know what your problem is, Ellen?" she'd asked after several short moments of contemplation.

"You mean, other than the huge flaw in my self-confidence and the total lack of sexual aggression?"

"In addition to those."

"Well, no, I guess don't know what my problem is, but I'm sure you'll tell me," she'd said as the phone rang again.

"You're too nice. That's your biggest problem. You take better care of everyone else than you do yourself. You're just too nice."

. . . Bananas. Vitamin C. Gourmet cat food. Canned peaches. Gourmet cat food. Tomato paste . . .

She *was* too nice. Vi was right, she thought, setting a box of denture paste on the belt and looking over the rack of impulse items to the man with the thick glasses. She should have left that old man panting and wheezing over his rusty lettuce and gone ahead of him in the line. She was there first. He'd offered to let her go first. But no. To be nice, she'd practically insisted that he go before her. Now she was out five hundred dollars *and* she was going to be late getting back to work.

She really was too nice. Wasting her lunch hour fetching groceries for old Mrs. Phipps when she could be across the street from the bank checking out the man in the camera shop.

She was way too darned nice! She was losing fifty cents an hour and a promotion to a girl with a tenth her experience. She had no place to spend her vacation this year. *And* she was going to have to hike all the way across the parking lot to her car on top of everything else.

She was almost angry about it, she decided with half a huff, squeezing a bag of cookies a little more forcefully than she might have otherwise, just for spite. Almost angry? What was that? she chastised herself. She had red hair. She was supposed to have a fiery temper. So where was it? Gathering a good head of angry steam was time-consuming; sustaining it was impossible for her. She was, quite likely, the only living redhead with a temper to match that of a dead blonde. It didn't seem fair.

That's when she saw it. Its little green cover seemed to flash at her like a neon sign. There it was between *Name Your Baby* and *Lose Ten Pounds Overnight*, below *Toilet Training Your Cat* and *Know Your Lucky Number* and above *Eat Yourself Healthy*. There it was. *Have It Your Way*, with a subtitle of *Getting What You Want*.

Granted, it was one of those five-inch mini-books that everyone sees and no one with any sense ever buys, but there it was, bright green cover, bold white lettering. *Have It Your Way*.

As if a book that size could tell her how to change her life, she thought with great disdain, looking first at the cashier, then at the woman behind her.

Ridiculous, she thought, reaching out to take a copy of *Word Find*, looking around once again. Her nice problem was a major disorder. She fanned the pages with a fake interest and put the booklet back. There was also that lack of sexual aggression and the flaw in her self-confidence. What she needed was an intense psychological overhaul. Not a pamphlet. Casually she ran her fingers through her hair. It would be absolutely insane to believe the solutions to her problems could be found in . . .

She flipped a copy of *Have It Your Way* in with Mrs. Phipps's groceries.

"Whoa! Hang on there. Let me give you a hand with that," said a male voice as Ellen wrestled with a splitting grocery bag full of dairy products and fresh produce beside her car in the parking lot behind the bank. She grabbed a carton of eggs with one hand and tucked an orange under her chin with the other. "Here we go. We've got it now."

Wedged between the backseat of the car and the open door, she couldn't see the man's face, but she was grateful to feel the extra set of hands laboring with hers to save her perishables.

"Oh, thank you," she said, flustered. "Why don't they double-bag the fruit?" she wanted to know, thrusting a stalk of celery under her arm as she guided the precarious pile of edibles back toward the seat she'd taken it from. "They double-bag canned goods. Why don't they double-bag the fruit? Which is going to make a bigger mess if you drop it?"

There was a soft laugh but no answer as the groceries toppled onto the seat in a heap. She pushed a thick tress of crimson curls to the back of her head in one frustrated gesture, then turned to thank her champion.

Her heart jumped and all but fell to the asphalt with a loud splat. It was him. The mystery man from across the street. The mercenary/war hero/spy/FBI guy/loving son or nephew that no one seemed to know anything about—aside from the fact that he was darkly handsome and built like a well-paid, high-class bouncer. She felt as awkward as a teenager with a new set of braces. Smile or run? She wished the earth would open wide and swallow her whole. Why him? Why now?

He gave her a tentative smile and a sympathetic look as he totally misinterpreted her reaction to him.

"One of those days, huh? I've had 'em," he said with friendly understanding. "You get out of bed in the morning, and from then on things run steadily from bad to worse." He grinned, and her heart flopped around pathetically in her chest. "Doesn't seem to be anything you can do to stop it either."

The sound of his voice echoed in her ears as the silence between them grew uncomfortably long. Her mind scrambled for a pithy response.

"No," she said.

"Well, a day only lasts so long," he said, preparing to go on his way again—out of her life. "And every new day is a fresh start. Tomorrow will be better."

"Yes," she said, once again dazzling him with her wit. He nodded and turned, walking with a slow, easy stride around the side of the building, toward the busy street.

"Tomorrow has got to be better," she added, tossing a loose block of cheese atop the bags of vegetables scattered across her backseat.

She took a deep breath, closed her eyes, and screamed silently in her soul. It was sweltering in the car, but rather than leaving her enervated as usual, the heat now seemed fuel the irrational excitement she felt as she probed the bottom of the bag for the answer to all her problems.

It was so little. She fanned the pages skeptically, flipped to the last page. . . .

This step-by-step procedure can be applied to any area of your life that you find dissatisfying. Try it. On your boss. On your coworkers. On your neighbors. On that special someone who has recently caught your eye. Just remember, being happy is your right, but it's up to you to exercise it.

Her brows lifted and her head bobbed up and down with the reasonableness of these statements. Slowly she turned to the first page and started to read.

> *You have the right to be happy. This is your new mantra. Say it. "I have the right to be happy." The Declaration of Independence guarantees you the right to "life, liberty, and the pursuit of happiness." So, if you're alive, liberate yourself and start pursuing whatever it is that will make you happy.*
>
> *You can have your own way. It's easy. All you have to do is want it badly enough. Ignoring your right to be happy is an inclination that is learned in early childhood. A time when so many of our attempts to explore our world, to seek out and satisfy our own happiness, are thwarted, and the altered behavior is rewarded with the approval and satisfaction of others. Ignoring our right to be happy is simply a bad habit we've learned.*
>
> *It's time to unlearn a bad habit. Break it. Replace it with the practice of having it your way and getting what you want. . . .*

No one seemed to notice she was thirty minutes late getting back from lunch. She hurried across the lobby to her desk, put her purse in the bottom drawer, and picked up her pen to look busy.

She had a clear view of most of the bank from her seat—the tellers in their booths, the drive-by window behind them, the glassed-in offices of the bank officers. She, Vi, and Delores Shoot were lined up a few feet from the front windows in small, low-walled cubicles to show the community that customer service was a high priority at Quincey First Federal Bank.

Quincey, Indiana, was a just-right place to live. Ellen had always thought so anyway. Not too small or intrusive. Not too big or impersonal. There were plenty of strangers in town, people she'd never seen before, to keep life interesting. People she recognized but didn't know, to keep it comfortable. There were acquaintances she could stop and talk to in the street, to keep it friendly. And since she'd grown up there, she had friends and family there too.

It was an unpretentious, middle-class American town, homespun and humble, and if she sometimes found it a bit boring and repetitive, she almost always assumed responsibility for her discontent. She had her faults, but shirking responsibility wasn't one of them. There were days when she felt responsible for everything—the weather, the national deficit, the lives of her customers. . . .

Mostly she checked on checks for people. "I can't believe I forgot to write down the amount," they'd say. "Now I have checks bouncing all over town." Frequently she'd pull up on her computer the balance of a savings account or trust fund or the maturity date of a specific money market CD. "We're planning a trip to Jamaica for our anniversary," someone would tell her. "I'm getting so excited and nervous. I just need to make sure we have enough money saved and that nothing goes wrong." On occasion she was forced to call a customer about insufficient funds. "I got the notices in the mail," would come a sad voice. "But my husband is still out of work, and since I got laid off it's been hard for us. I have three children. They have to eat. I have to keep them warm. Can't we work something out?"

How could anyone not respond to someone else's embarrassments? Their concerns and worries? Their desperation?

Today her phone was unusually quiet. The people of Quincey were coping. Her sigh was one of relief and gratification, fringed with a bit of boredom.

You got used to working in a fishbowl, she mused, glancing out the large display window. Being on exhibit all day, it became second nature to keep your hands as far from your nose as possible, to sit with your knees together, and to adjust your bra straps and panty hose in the ladies' room only.

The world passed by that big window all day long, and one hardly considered it. She suspected it was the same from the other side as well. Who paid any attention to people working in the window of a bank when they were busy living their own lives?

Ellen took a good hard look out the smudge-free glass. The camera shop was directly across the street from her desk, its windows shiny clean. Poster enlargements of a boy with his dog, a blushing bride, and a stream in the woods took up most of the space above a small display of cameras, cases, and tripods.

What was he doing in there? she wondered, leaning back in her chair, her pen bumping rhythmically against her upper lip. Developing film? Unpacking new stock? Flexing his muscles?

Then, as if in answer to her reflections, he appeared in the glass doorway. Resting his hands on the push bar, he looked up the street and down, then directly across into her cubicle.

Her heart stopped and she sat perfectly still. He looked straight into her eyes, entered her soul without knocking. She held her breath. Then he was smiling, and her heart took off, beating too fast; her nerves twitched to life under her skin. She hunched her shoulders over her desk, kept her head down in deep concentration, and tried to gather her thoughts.

Had he seen her? Had he really smiled at her?

"Vi?" she called out, louder than her telephone voice but not so loud as to disturb the dignified fiscal quiet maintained in the bank.

"I saw it," Vi whispered back loudly. "He smiled at me." Something twisted painfully in Ellen's chest. "Maybe I won't have to buy that camera after all. Maybe he'll come open an account."

"Maybe," Ellen said, swallowing the envy she felt. Vi was always so confident, always so sure. Ellen should have known that smile wasn't for her.

She tossed the pen onto the desk and leaned back again in her chair. *Why* hadn't that smile been for her? Hadn't she reacted to it as if it had been? She turned her head to the window. The man was gone, but she could still see him standing there, smiling. She pursed her lips and her gaze meandered slowly to the bottom drawer of her desk.

Determine exactly what it is you want. You can't have your way unless you know which way you want to go. Be practical. Be realistic. Reach for the stars . . . but stay in your own galaxy.

He was definitely in her galaxy. On her planet even, earthy and human. He'd helped her with her groceries. It was possible that smile had been for her. Vi didn't have a monopoly on happiness; she wasn't the only one who could take what they wanted from the world. Her gaze gravitated toward the teller boxes across the room and settled on Lisa Lee, earning fifty cents more an hour in a position she was barely trained for, knowing full well that if she played her cards right, she was in line to move up the line ahead of Ellen.

No, she wasn't being fair.

Lisa was a sweet girl, a Korean immigrant who'd come to Quincey with her husband to make a better life for themselves. She worked hard—on her English, in her citizenship classes, at her duties at the bank. Ellen liked her . . . but . . . well, the position of loan officer was in her galaxy too. She worked hard too.

Okay. She'd had enough.

She knew exactly what she wanted now. Change. And she was going to make it happen. Was she not the captain of her own vessel? Was it not her life to direct? Could she not create her own destiny? If being too nice was causing her to fall short of her targets, wasn't it time to try new trajectories? Wasn't it her responsibility, as well as her right, to make her own happiness?

And it wasn't the job or the money or the man— none of them in themselves had the power to make her happy—but *knowing* would. *Knowing* that she could have the promotion and the pay raise, and the man, if she wanted them—now, that would make her happy. *Knowing* that she could change her life, that she wasn't a victim of fate, that being too nice was a curable disease—that would make her happy.

She'd get a pay raise, she'd get the promotion, and she'd make that man smile at her. *Her*—in a way that left no doubt in anyone's mind as to whom he was smiling at, in a significant way that would curl her toes and cause her to smile right back at him. That's what she wanted. That would make her happy. And she had a right to be happy.

"Vi," she said, the wheels on her chair squeaking a

little as she pushed herself away from her desk and reached into her bottom drawer for her purse.

"Yeah?"

"Have you ever had one of those days when your life didn't seem to be worth living, and then something"—she held the small green booklet in both hands—"some little thing happens, and everything is different?"

Across the street in the camera shop, Jonah Blake was contemplating the short-term emotional benefits and the long-term physical drawbacks to putting another dent in the wall with his forehead.

He growled out loud, then took a deep breath, holding it until he was calm enough to blow it out slowly. A half-crazed laugh escaped him as he shook his fists at the ceiling.

"Jonah, old buddy, this town and that woman are going to drive you over the edge if you're not careful," he told himself, blowing yet another pent-up breath out through stiff lips.

He scanned the shop, looking for something to do, searching for something to focus his attention on—other than the woman in the window across the street. But it just wasn't going to happen. Nothing had changed since the last time he scanned the shop, looking for something to do, searching for something to focus his attention on.

He'd processed every strip of film he could find, developed the pictures, gathered them up, put them in envelopes, filed them in alphabetical order. He'd washed the windows, wiped off the display cases, dusted the cameras. He'd vacuumed the floor, retallied the negative balance in the books four times, done fifty push-ups in the back room, and that was all before lunch.

Since then, he'd been kicking himself stupid for acting like a tongue-tied idiot when he'd finally gotten an opportunity to talk to her. "Duh. One of those days, huh?" he muttered to himself and cringed, remembering. Not the most intriguing opening line he'd ever used.

Not that he'd actually used all that many opening lines for a man his age. To date, his dealings with women had been long-term sexual encounters at best, with very little emotional involvement. And to be truthful, they'd suited him just fine.

Which wasn't to say that on rare occasions he hadn't contemplated the efforts involved in meeting a different kind of woman; in allowing himself to feel something for her; in marriage and children. Those occasions had left him feeling empty, alone, and small, and were often best avoided. But deep down inside, he knew that was exactly what he'd always wanted. To grow up, marry a nice woman, have children, and spend the rest of his life loving and taking care of them. Trouble was, he had no idea of where to start to build this dream he had.

His own childhood had been fragmented. What he hadn't deliberately forgotten was blurry and permeated with sadness and confusion. What he did remember had little to do with home and family, and a lot to do with discipline and control, regulation and achievement.

He'd grown up in a man's world, and while women had certainly topped the list of topics for conversation and were the ultimate prize on a Saturday night, they had remained—for him—bizarre, alien beings who were difficult to talk to, uncomfortable to be with, and hard to understand.

Except for this one . . .

The first time he'd seen her, with all that dark red hair glinting sparks of copper in the afternoon sun, the bright white dress with the green trim, the long legs that looked as if they started somewhere near her neck—he hadn't been able to take his eyes off her.

She'd come out of the bank and stood holding the door open for an elderly couple coming out behind her, a frail-looking woman pushing a man in a wheelchair. The wheels had gotten stuck on the threshold. She hadn't been able to make the woman grasp backing up to let her back in to help, and she hadn't been able to get help from inside the bank. Jonah had thought about sprinting across the street to help her, but instead he'd watched her walk briskly down the street, turn the corner, and re-enter the bank from the rear—because soon she was gently talking the old woman into giving up control of the chair, tipping it back slightly to pass over the threshold, and pushing it out onto the sidewalk.

She could have left them there and considered her duty done. Instead, she'd made Jonah smile as he watched her wave the couple good-bye and then stand there watching them doubtfully. He'd seen the concern come to her face as they crawled at a snail's pace toward their car; saw it scrunch up with fear and dread as the woman came incredibly close to ramming the man's chair into a too-small space between a parking meter and a streetlight pole. He was completely enraptured by the time she sighed and rushed once more to their aid, helping first the old man then the old woman into their car, folding the wheelchair into the trunk, and standing on the curb with a furrowed brow as they drove away.

He couldn't remember the last time he'd seen someone go to so much trouble for someone else. The patience, the kindness, the concern. And he was pretty sure they weren't relatives, as there had been no farewell kisses or hugs, just polite friendly smiles and an obvious mutual deference between them.

Since then he'd watched her working diligently, smiling and shaking hands respectfully with the people who came to see her, fetching coffee for some, always making an effort to put them at ease.

He liked her, liked the way she looked, but more, liked the way small kindnesses seemed second nature to her. He liked that she took her time and dealt with people slowly and gently and thoughtfully. He liked that she didn't fiddle with her hair all day, or file her nails in her spare time. He liked the way her face lit up when she smiled, and he tried a thousand times to imagine what her laughter would sound like . . . and her voice . . . or a pleasured moan in the back of her throat. . . .

In fact, the only thing he couldn't like about her was that she was so unconscious of the world outside her window that she rarely looked in his direction. When she left the bank at six every evening, her long legs carried her with purposeful strides, in a hurry, and she never seemed to see him loitering around the parking lot, trying to catch her eye.

Then the gods had smiled on him twice in one day. First in the parking lot behind the bank, when he was so dumbstruck and awkward that the second time, when he caught her looking out the bank window and smiled at her, she leaned over her desk and pretended not to see him.

His sigh was a mixture of boredom and frustration—one of the most explosive mixtures known to man.

If *she* were a man, he'd know exactly how to proceed to engage her trust and win her friendship and loyalty. He was used to dealing with men, who were so uncomplicated, who took most things at face value. You didn't have to bathe or shave or wear clean clothes to have a good time with them. Men were easy to understand. Women were as convoluted as feather collectors in hurricane country. They didn't make any sense at all.

Restlessly his eyes wandered slowly over the wall across from where he stood at the register. The old black-and-white photographs in cheap black frames, hanging in an uneven line, were a constant reminder of why he'd come to Quincey in the first place.

A single disbelieving laugh broke loose in his chest. Why was he so surprised? Everything but the clocks seemed to be working against him in the queer little town. He was running a camera shop he knew nothing about. He couldn't leave. He couldn't get a pretty woman to look his way to save his soul. He couldn't even gloat in the face of the dying man he'd hated all his life.

CHAPTER TWO

STEP TWO

Alter your life by altering your attitudes.
—William James

Success is ninety percent attitude. And attitude is the mind-set or outlook you have and project in regard to any given person, place, thing, or idea. Assume a mental position toward what you want. You deserve it. It's yours. No one can do it better than you. It's your destiny. Show your surprise if anyone thinks otherwise. . . .

"I'm surprised by your attitude, Ellen," Joleen Powers said, smiling and nodding. The middle-aged office manager in pressed pleats and sensible shoes had also been surprised by her sudden request for a private conference moments before the bank closed for the day. At first leery, she realized that Ellen had come to her with good news rather than bad and was now considerably more relaxed. "I had no idea you were interested in learning Mary's job. And like you say, there's no one here more qualified than you. To tell you the truth, I just assumed you were content in Bonds and Trusts." She laughed at herself. "I should have guessed you were more ambitious than that, and just too polite to say so. I've been meaning to tell you how well you're doing in Customer Service, as well, and how much we appreciate you helping out there when you're not busy. It takes a lot of patience. Not everyone can handle the patrons with such consistent courtesy. Even Mr. Bragg noticed how well you were working out in both departments, so I'm sure he'll include you in any decisions he makes about—"

"Then maybe he won't be amazed to hear that I want a raise too," Ellen said, nervously firing off her statement too soon, her heart thumping away at a dizzying speed, her hands cold and clammy with sweat. *You deserve it. It's yours.* The little green book with the bold white title weighed heavily in the pocket of her jacket as she watched the expression change on Joleen's face.

"A raise? Well, of course, you'll be making a little more in Loans if . . ." Her voice trailed off as Ellen began to shake her head.

"In my present position," she said, stunned to hear the words squeeze by the lump of pure raw nerve in her throat, "I manage all of Trusts and Bonds and spend a great deal of time on costumer service. Except for you and Mary, I've been here longer than anyone else. I haven't taken a sick day in three years. I come in on my days off to fill in. I'm a good employee, Joleen. You know I am."

"I'm not denying it, Ellen. I haven't had or heard one complaint about you since the day you started here. It's just that a raise right now—"

"A fifty-one-cents-an-hour raise," someone using her mouth and body interjected. Truly, she felt possessed. Never in her wildest dreams had she imagined herself saying such things.

Obviously this sort of behavior from her had never occurred in Joleen's dreams either, as she frowned and looked somewhat perplexed.

"Fifty-one? Ellen, that's a big jump. We don't normally give raises in increments of more than two or three percent."

"It's not nearly as big a jump as my leaving and going to work at Quincey's First Savings and Loan, or People's Bank." Hysterical laughter bubbled in her chest. Where were these words coming from? If she didn't discover the source soon, and stop them, she'd talk herself out of a job altogether.

"Oh now, there's no need for that," Joleen said quickly. She stood and walked over to the filing cabinet. "I'm sure we can work this out. When was your last pay raise? You know, I don't recall offhand . . ."

"Two years ago. Last year you said no one was getting one because of the low interest rates," she said as the panic in her heart reached its peak, and she completely missed the worried concern in Joleen's expression.

"Yes, yes. I remember that. So you're about due for another evaluation anyway, right?"

"Possibly. I do know I'm due for a raise." Why back down now? Her heart was going to stop any second and she'd be dead. What difference would it make?

"My goodness, yes," Joleen said, breezing through the papers in the folder as if she were actually reading them. "I believe you are due for a raise. Long overdue, in fact."

"I am?" Ellen asked. "I mean . . . yes. I am. Over-due. Long . . . in fact . . . overdue."

Dear God. Had it worked? Was it over? Was that all there was to it? So simple. Keep repeating what you want to the person you want it from, until you think you might die, and then . . . it happens? No, that sounded more like nagging. This was different. This was sticking to her guns. This was being right about something and knowing it and sticking it out to the end. Not backing down, not showing weakness, not be-ing too understanding or too nice. This was getting what she wanted.

However . . .

"I appreciate you looking into this for me, Joleen," she said, feeling more herself and seeing, at last, the discomfort in the woman's eyes. "If I came on a little strong or sounded like I didn't appreciate all you've done for me over the years, I—"

"Oh, no, Ellen, not at all," Joleen said, a tentative smile on her face. "You were right to come to me. You've been with us a long time. You're a good em-ployee. We want you to be happy here."

"I am happy here," she said, a whole lot happier than she had been. And to try out her newfound power once more, she added, "I'll be even happier if you give me a chance in Loans."

"Well, I can't think of one good reason not to, now that I know you're interested. And by coming to me like this today, you've certainly demonstrated your confi-dence and leadership skills. I think you'd be an excellent addition to the Loans Department."

Confidence and leadership skills. She almost laughed as she let herself out of Joleen's office a few minutes later. It amused her to think of the utter waste of breath it was to use those words to describe her—but wouldn't the look on Vi's face have been priceless if she'd heard them? Confidence and leadership skills. She wrote the words on a slip of paper at her desk, then wrote *Ellen Webster* beside them. This time she did chuckle. Incongruous at first, they began to look good together, like polar opposites, like the symbol for yin and yang.

Nodding with satisfaction, she swiveled her chair toward the window, toward her next experiment. She sighed. Getting the man to smile at her as if she were the only woman on earth wasn't going to be as easy, or even as justifiable, as getting her pay raise. It wasn't as if it were her right or as if she'd done something to deserve any special attention from him. But there was a principle here, a point she wanted to make, a central idea she needed to prove to herself.

It was something she wanted. It would make her happy to know she could have it if she wanted it. And it was her right to be happy.

And what about the man, she thought, taking her purse from the bottom drawer and scanning her desk for neatness before she left for the day. Would he mind being her unwitting partner in her testing of the little green book? Would he understand a lifetime of giving with little reward? Of helping others across the finish line and inevitably coming in last? Would he understand her need to take control of her life, to place her own hopes and desires first for a change?

She left the bank by the front door, eyeing the camera shop as she circled around to the parking lot in back. Was it fair of her to involve him at all? Maybe he had problems of his own. What if he . . . ? No. She was being too nice again. Look at Vi, she consoled herself. She didn't know any four-letter words like *can't* or *won't* or *don't* or *stop* or *wait* or *fair*. Her life was her own. She took what she wanted. She was happy.

Ellen stopped at the end of the building before turning the corner and glanced back at the camera shop. All the man had to do was smile at her—just her, in a special way—was that so much to ask of him?

"Is something wrong?"

She startled and backed up against the red brick of the bank, watching with wide eyes as the man squinted at his own camera shop in an effort to see whatever it was that had held her attention so long.

"I don't see anything. Did you see something over there?" he asked, too delighted that the gods had not given up on him to worry much about a bunch of cameras. Giving her time to recover her wits, he went on, "If it's a burglar, he's going to be disappointed. There's twenty bucks and a roll of antacids in the till, and he'll have to stay up all night rubbing the serial numbers off the cameras before he can pawn them. Not a very smart burglar. He could do a lot better than a failing camera shop. Not a wise choice."

"No," she said, trying to smile and breathe at the same time, and doing both badly. "I mean, no, I didn't see anyone in your shop." She hesitated. She liked his eyes. They would have been plain old hazel green eyes in someone else, but in this man they were alive with light and perception—like a pair of mystical stones from another time and place. "But then, no, you're right too. Robbing a camera shop wouldn't be as profitable as robbing . . . oh, say . . . the bank across the street from it."

He grinned.

There. She'd won her prize, and the butterflies in

her stomach were a testament. Or was that simply an impersonal smile of amusement? She could see immediately that further experimentation would be necessary to determine exactly when he was smiling a smile meant specifically for her.

"But then, robbing isn't a wise occupation to begin with, so . . ." Her voice trailed off as she suddenly realized that she'd painted herself into a corner with a lame topic of conversation. What could she possibly say to him now? She'd never get that smile if she let him walk away once more thinking her completely devoid of intelligent conversation.

Alter your life by altering your attitudes. Attitude is mind-set. You deserve it. It's yours.

"Ah . . . but . . . I'm glad I ran into you. I . . . I didn't thank you earlier for helping me. I was already late getting back to work. I could have been chasing oranges all over the parking lot if you hadn't come along."

"I'm glad I was there," he said, patting his pockets, reaching into one without looking away from her. "I was hoping to run into you, too, actually. I found these in the shop and thought you might be able to use them." He held up a wad of crumpled plastic bags. "You still need to get those groceries out of your car somehow."

Smiling, she glanced from the bags to his face. "I do. I . . ." The smoldering light in his eyes held her, mesmerized her. Her mind was a blank. "I . . . Thank you. It was kind of you to think of me. Thank you very much." Stunned stupid, she took the bags. "I really appreciate this."

There. A stranger being nice to her for no reason at all. And what did he know about her? Only what he'd seen that morning—she'd been ill-tempered and rude. Being too nice never intrigued men like him—anger and frustration had caught his attention. *Success is ninety percent attitude.* And hadn't she just seen that in Joleen's office? And wasn't the man impressed with it?

He shrugged. "They were laying around. I stuffed them in my pocket in case I saw you again." He'd never been good at pussyfooting. "Actually, I could have just tied them to the door handle of your car, but I've been pacing the parking lot waiting for you to come out."

"You have?" She vacillated between fear and excitement. She hoped neither reaction showed on her face.

"I was hoping I could talk you into having dinner with me sometime."

"Me?" she asked, speaking before she could untangle her thoughts. He was more than impressed by her new attitude, he was attracted to it. Excitement churned in her belly. Endless possibilities were lining up in the back of her mind.

He nodded, then glanced about uncomfortably. "I'm sorry. I'm not very good at things like this. I'm used to taking the direct approach, which puts me at a distinct disadvantage in the subtle art of pursuing women. But the fact is, I've been wanting to meet you for a while, and if I don't ask you out now, I may not be able to come up with another good excuse to talk to you."

Pursuing women? *He* wanted to pursue *her*? She stared at him for a second or two, then laughed. "Well, that certainly is a direct approach," she said, turning and walking slowly toward the parking lot. Be cool. Be blasé, she thought, adjusting her attitude. Men pick you up like this all the time. She added a little extra swing to her walk—it couldn't hurt. "I, on the other hand, have been wondering if I can afford a fancy camera that's too complicated for me to work. Not one of the self-doing-everything kind that a monkey could work, mind you—I wouldn't want you to think I was stupid—but a really, really complicated one I'd have to keep taking back to your shop to figure out."

Okay, so it was Vi's idea, but she'd been invited to tag along. And it *could* have been her idea if she weren't afflicted with a lack of confidence, a sexual aggression deficit, and being too darned nice for her own good. The camera tactic would have occurred to her eventually, if she'd had the right attitude at the time.

A slow, knowing grin spread across his face and sent tingling chills up her spine.

"Very clever," he said, smiling his approval. He should have known she would make this easy for him. She was too nice to let him feel awkward and uncomfortable for very long. In mock despair, he added, "And I could have used that sale. Plus we could have spent days together, because I don't know one end of a camera from the other."

"You don't?"

"Nope. My camera is the self-doing-everything kind that a monkey can work." She laughed. The sound satisfied his soul from one end to the other. "I'm not even a very good photographer. I get a lot of shots of my thumb and headless people; friends with fire in their eyes and overexposed vistas I barely recognize. But I can process film like *that*," he said, snapping his fingers in the air. "And that appears to be the moneymaking end of the business anyway, so . . ."

"So, you do know one end of a camera from the other."

"No," he said, chuckling. "Not really. There are a

couple of machines over there with A-B-C directions on them that do all the work. I just feed the film into one to be processed, then feed the processed film into the other one for prints, and put the prints in envelopes. It's a no-brain operation . . . until someone comes in for an enlargement or to buy a camera. Then it's an acting career."

Again she laughed and decided then and there that she liked this man. They had arrived at her car when she turned, saying, "My name's Ellen Webster." From habit, she held out her hand.

He glanced down before taking it. "Jonah Blake," he said, noting her expression as their grasps fit together comfortably like cold feet and thick socks on a midwinter night.

"Are you Mr. Blake's son or nephew?" Inquiring minds would want to know tomorrow during coffee break.

"I'm his son," he said, a curious aspect to the tone of his voice as he continued to hold her hand. He liked the feel of it. Not frail but not too big or too strong. Not controlling. Capable and soothing perhaps. Gentle and sensitive.

"And are you an FBI agent or a spy? A mercenary or a national hero?" she asked, smiling as he first frowned and then started to laugh, her hand slipping from his. "You haven't talked to many people in town, so we've had to make up our own stories about you."

"I see," he said, chuckling. "So now I can either make up some fabulous lie and bask in my fifteen minutes of fame, or I can tell you the truth and slip helplessly into the pit of the boring and mundane. What a choice."

He was joking, of course. There was nothing about

him that said he thought himself boring or mundane. Self-contained maybe, and judicious if the caution in his eyes was any indicator. But boring? No.

"Or you could dodge all the questions and remain a mystery," she said, enhancing the last word as she popped the lock on her car door. "I can't remember the last time a real live, genuine man of mystery wandered into Quincey."

"But . . . could a real live, genuine mystery man persuade you to have dinner with him tonight?"

For fun, she bit her bottom lip and studied him with narrowed eyes, taking her time, enjoying the view, elated by the sense of power and danger surging through her veins.

"Yeah. I think he could," she said, the little critters in her belly belying the sanguine smile on her lips. It was also a bit Vi-like to be so obvious about her attraction to him but . . . in for a penny . . . why shy away now? "Does he like Italian food?"

"Yes."

"Does he know where Amherst Street is?"

"He can find it."

"Seven-twenty-one West," she said, glancing at her watch. "Apartment 2B. At eight?"

She gave her name, rank, and serial number without making him ask. She set the time so he didn't have to worry about giving her enough to get ready. Picked the restaurant even. Could anything be simpler than that? He was falling fast and hard for this woman. She was all the good things a woman was supposed to be, with a simple uncomplicated mind like a man's.

"I'll be there," he said, grinning his satisfaction at his fantastic find. "With or without cloak and dagger?"

She returned his grin. "Your choice," she said, sliding into the car and swinging the door closed.

He'd never known anything like the feeling in his chest as he watched her start up the car, put it in gear, and drive off with a quick wave. Was this love? This I-don't-care-if-I'm-not-breathing-I've-never-felt-better feeling that was making him light-headed and weak—was that it? Or was it the pressure building underneath it? The overwhelming fear of both winning and losing at once.

He forced himself to breathe deeply as he strode across the lot to the car he'd leased when he'd first arrived in town. A provisional act that now clashed with a strange, isolated desire for some sort of permanence in his life. He frowned and shook his head. Permanence? What was happening to him?

Ellen couldn't recall the drive home as anything but a blur of hazy what-if's and should-I's. What if she'd been too forward? What if, now that he'd spoken to her, he was rethinking his interest in her? Should she use more or less attitude when he showed up that night? Should she get all dressed up or play it casual? What if she slipped up? What if he really was some sort of mercenary killer? Should she tell him the truth and forget this charade? What if he found out that she was simply too nice, with hardly any attitude at all? What if . . .

"Oh no." She groaned aloud as she approached the old Victorian house on Amherst Street. She occupied one of the four apartments the elegant old place afforded, with its single turret and scalloped friezes and porch brackets. A dented, paint-chipped, rear-taillight-hanging Mazda was parked out front, one wheel well over the curb and twisted into the lawn.

A small nagging headache commenced as she pulled into her parking space behind the house. A sort of sad frustration filled her as she rubbed her forehead with the tips of her fingers. Her brother, Felix, was the single greatest drain on her patience and goodwill. As the only son and most beloved youngest sibling in her family, Felix looked like a twenty-three-year-old man but often acted like a spoiled twelve-year-old.

"Can we help you with those groceries, dear?" came Mrs. Phipps's weak but still shrill voice from the screened porch that served as the back entrance. "We've been watching for you. We feel just awful asking you to pick up so much this time. We were out of everything. You are such a dear, sweet girl."

It never mattered if it was a box of frozen broccoli or eight bags of groceries, Mrs. Phipps stood on the porch and said the exact same thing every evening.

"No, Mrs. Phipps. You stay put. I can handle this. There's not much here," she said, as she always did. "How are you today?"

"Well, we're better now that we know you're home safe and sound. We heard on the news about a woman in Lafayette who had her car stolen while she was still in it. Can you imagine? They put a pistol in her face, told her to get out, drove off with her car."

"Carjacking, Mrs. Phipps," she said, her head inside the car, her words muffled, as she gathered up groceries and stuffed them into the bags Jonah Blake had given her. "Welcome to the twentieth century."

"We're sorry, dear. We didn't hear that."

"I said," she shouted, "the grocery bag split wide open." Seeing her brother's car on the front lawn had shortened what little temper she had, and Mrs. Phipps was unfairly feeling the mild heat of it. To make up for her sarcasm, she added, "I sure do miss paper bags."

"Oh, yes. Paper bags. And you could use them for so many things. The garbage. Storage. When my son was little, we'd make pirate hats out of them, and I sometimes used them for dear Harold's lunches, you know, when he forgot his lunch box at work? We used them for book covers and to wrap packages for mailing and—"

"It's cooling off a bit, I think," Ellen said, or the endless uses of good old-fashioned brown paper grocery bags would have gone on endlessly. "Is your air conditioner keeping you cool enough?"

"Oh my, yes. But it does whir so. We suppose that can't be helped though, that whirring noise."

The *we* she spoke of was herself and her cat. He was as black as Beelzebub, but overweight and lazy. She called him Bubba.

"No, I don't suppose so," Ellen said, mounting the shallow steps, her arms laden with groceries. "We had Jim Penny come tinker with it, remember? He said it was supposed to make that noise."

"Yes, yes," Mrs. Phipps said, pushing the screen door open for her. Bubba sat dead center in the doorway. "We remember. That Jim Penny. I had him in my Sunday school class, years and years ago. Had ants in his pants. Just couldn't sit still."

Ellen chuckled at that and stepped over Bubba. These days, Jim Penny was slow as grass growing, taking weeks to finish the handyman jobs he was hired to do.

"Well, he wouldn't steer you wrong, Mrs. Phipps. If

Jim says your air conditioner is supposed to whir, it should whir."

"That's true. Jim never did lie. I'd ask who put food coloring in the baptismal font, and Jim would step right up." She hesitated and looked concerned. "Felix is upstairs in your apartment."

Ellen nodded, squeezing sideways though the back door. "I saw his car. How is he?"

"Well, he didn't stop to talk, so we suspect he's under the weather a bit," Mrs. Phipps said, her way of saying he was drunk as an empty teacup. "But we haven't heard one peep out of him since he went up, so maybe he's just sleeping."

"Most likely," Ellen muttered, entering the narrow hallway that led toward the front of the building and Mrs. Phipps's apartment.

"We'd best leave him sleep and have our tea."

Mrs. Phipps was tiny, maybe five feet tall before her shoulders had bowed and her spine had curved with age. Gray haired and thin skinned, she was always impeccably dressed in a floral shirtdress with the belt cinched at the approximate middle of her tiny frame— and she always had hot water on for tea.

"Umm . . . maybe not tonight, Mrs. Phipps," Ellen said, finding it hard to deny the old lady anything. Her too-nice syndrome was acutely susceptible to anything old, young, sick, or fuzzy. She was aware of this. She would have to be strong. "It's been sort of a strange day for me."

"Oh dear," Mrs. Phipps said, looking concerned and hugely disappointed at the same time. "Bad strange or good strange? You know, there's nothing like a little tea and a little sympathy to smooth out the edges of a strange day."

Ellen chuckled softly, heaving the bags of groceries and the ten-pound bag of kitty litter onto the counter near the sink.

"I know," she said. "But this has actually been sort of a good strange day, and it isn't over yet, so . . . I really do have to go."

She started for the door.

"Maybe it's just as well," she heard the old lady say. "We've run out of Earl Grey, I'm afraid. We were going to have to have chamomile with rose hips, and we know that's not your favorite. But we're all out of the other."

"I'll pick some up tomorrow."

It was out of her mouth before she could think to stop it, and once again she was committed to going to the grocery store during her lunch break or after work the next day. And it wasn't as though she didn't know what was happening.

"You're such a dear. Truly, we don't know what we'd do without you, Ellen. If only we had some of those cream-filled ladyfinger cookies. Then our tea tomorrow would be perfect. Oh! And a loaf of thin-sliced bread too. We'll have watercress. We know you're always hungrier after work than you let on."

This was Mrs. Phipps's modus operandi—casually mentioning, regretfully and repeatedly, her entire shopping list for the next day. They had operated very well this way for quite some time—but things were different now. She wasn't too nice anymore.

But dealing with Mrs. Phipps now would take all the time and energy she'd need to get Felix out of her apartment before her date arrived. And besides, Mrs. Phipps was old and sweet and harmless and cute. . . .

No, no. She was time-consuming, inconvenient,

bothersome, and repetitive, sometimes telling the same silly old story or reporting the same neighborhood news more than twice. She needed to be dealt with. Tomorrow, Mrs. Phipps would get attitude.

"Tell you what, Mrs. Phipps. Why don't you write up a list of all the things you might be needing for a while, and I'll stop by for it on my way to work in the morning."

"You are the nicest young woman, Ellen. And so good to us," she said, standing by her apartment door, looking a bit bewildered at the hasty departure.

"I know," Ellen muttered under her breath before smiling down over the banister at her. "See you later, Mrs. Phipps."

The old lady said something else and shut her door quietly, but Ellen hardly noticed. As she approached her apartment door, Bubba right behind her, she was searching for the anger she'd had not ten minutes earlier. She turned the knob, knowing it wouldn't be locked, and walked in.

Felix lay sprawled across her couch, his long, dishwater-blond hair cascading over the armrest, one arm across his chest and one dangling loose to the floor. His mouth hung open. His clothes were dirty and wrinkled.

A long, drawn-out snore was her only greeting. It struck her as a most horrible noise. Disgusting. Nasty and vulgar somehow. Far, far worse than any noise they'd ever made during the belching contests they used to have under the dining room table every Thanksgiving when they were kids. Her heart softened momentarily, remembering the little boy he'd once been—but then he snored again.

Bubba dallied about in the doorway, then judiciously backed away as she began to swing the door

back and forth by the knob and then slammed it closed
with all her might, rattling windows throughout the
house. She smiled and watched Felix's body jerk and
jump, rise inches off the couch, then fall and slide to the
floor. But by the time his eyes opened and he was groping to sit up, Bubba was crying at having a door rudely
slammed in his face and Ellen's countenance was stern
and angry once more.

"Oh. Hi," he said, as if he were surprised to see her;
as if she'd come to call unexpectedly. He flashed his
teeth in a would-be smile.

"Get off my floor," she said, her voice quiet but
sharp as a fresh razor blade. She leaned to one side to
open the door for Bubba, who had free run of the
house. "Get that hair out of your face and get out of my
apartment."

"Bad day at the office, honey?" he asked, his own
voice raspy and hungover.

"I had a great day at the office. Just a really lousy
homecoming."

"You mean," he paused to push the hair out of his
face and take a good look at her, "you're not tickled to
see me?"

"Not like this, no. Felix, you look awful."

He laughed. "You should see how I feel."

"No, thanks." She watched him make several feeble
attempts to hoist himself back onto the couch. He did
look pale. There were dark circles under his eyes; his
lips were dry and chapped. She shook her head and
sighed. "Why do you do this to yourself?"

He shrugged, his head in his hands, then reached
down to help fat Bubba up onto the couch beside him.

She tried to ignore the tugging at her heart as she
dropped her purse and jacket on the wing chair and

went into the small kitchen, returning with a bottle of aspirin and a glass of water. She held them out to him and, when he didn't take notice, kicked his foot. Squinting at the water as if he didn't recognize what it was, he reached for the bottle of pills.

"These'd go down better with a scotch." An icy silence. "Or a beer if you've got one. I don't want to put you out."

"You do," she said, setting the water on the side table where he could reach it. "You do put me out. Very much. Felix, it's bad enough that you're doing this to yourself, but I've told you before that I won't let you do it to me too. I don't want to see you like this. I don't want my neighbors seeing you like this . . . or your car parked on the front lawn. This is my home, not a flophouse. If you want help, I'll help you find some, but I'm not going to tolerate you just—"

"I do. I do," he said, repeating it several times before she actually heard it. "I do need help."

Well . . . okay. The man, the smile, and the little green book were immediately pushed out of mind. If a sober and responsible life was a star in her brother's galaxy, a star he was reaching for, then her stars could wait awhile. She'd do everything she could to push him a little closer to his goals.

"Felix," she said, the awe in her evident. "That's wonderful." She laughed. "Where do we start? I've been waiting for you to make this decision, and I'm so unprepared." She made a couple of false starts, then decided on the phone book. "A rehab clinic. That's what we need, don't you think?" She sat on her jacket in the wing chair, fanning the pages, prattling. "M-N-O-P . . . I'm so proud of you, Felix. You'll never regret this. They have trained professionals in these places. Know all the tricks. All the best ways to do this. I feel like crying, I'm so happy you've decided to do this. R-R-Ra-Re . . ."

"Elly. Elly. I need help. Not a clinic."

"Oh. A twelve-step program, then. I think they follow some sort of similar program in these clinics and there's more moral support, but if you—"

"Ellen! Drinking is not my problem." He stood up quickly, jostling Bubba and cringing briefly from the pressure in his head. He glared at his sister. "You and Jane both think that if I stop drinking, my life is going to turn into some sort of fairy tale where I run around in a suit of armor and ride a white horse and save maidens, and nothing but good things will happen to me. But the truth is, my drinking is the only armor I've got. I'm a screwup, Ellen. I always have been. Everything I touch turns rotten."

"That's not true."

"Yes, it is. I was a screwup in high school. I couldn't finish college. Couldn't hold my marriage together. Can't hold down a job—"

"Because you drink."

"Because I'm a screwup!" he shouted emphatically. "Drinking is the only way I can survive. People feel sorry for drunks. They let them get away with murder." As an afterthought, he added, "Almost."

"That's crazy."

He scoffed, "Oh yeah? If I were stone sober and sitting around the empty apartment I got out of my divorce settlement, with no job and no prospects, you think Mom would give me money to pay the rent? You think my friends would buy my drinks, or would they expect me to buy my own? Think my gambling buddies would let me ride as long as they have if I had a job?

Heck no! But I'm sick, see? So Mom gives me money. My friends buy my drinks. And I have gambling debts that *you*, big sister," he said, pointing a shaky finger at her, "would not believe. So don't be telling me my problem is drinking. I drink just fine. My problem is— I'm a screwup."

Staring, openmouthed and dazed, she started to shake her head.

"Felix, can you hear yourself talking?"

He snorted a half laugh and fell back down onto the couch. Bubba opened one eye and rolled with the bounce. "Question is, can you hear what I'm saying?"

"Yes," she said, slapping the phone book closed on her lap. "You owe someone money and you're scared."

He giggled insanely. "I owe a lot of people money." He fought with the cap on the aspirin bottle. "But I'm only scared of the big ugly ones. Can you open this for me?"

CHAPTER THREE

STEP THREE

The first problem is not to learn, but to unlearn.
—Gloria Steinem

*You're unhappy with the present course of your life. So,
turn left and go that way. Everything we think we
know has either been told to us or learned through trial
and error. Think about the choices you make. Is vanilla
ice cream really the best? Or is it the most readily
available? Or is it what your mother always served for
dessert? When was the last time you tried Rocky Road?
Maple nut? Cherry Garcia? If what you're doing isn't
making you happy, try doing the exact opposite.*

She was a failure. She hadn't taken two steps in the
little green book and already she could feel herself slipping back into her old ways. First with Mrs. Phipps.
Then with Felix. At this rate she'd end up being too
nice for the rest of her life.

She wrapped a towel around her wet head, cinched

her terry robe at the waist, and sighed at the distorted reflection in the steamy mirror. Whoever had written that little book obviously hadn't anticipated the likes of Mrs. Phipps and Felix. The exact opposite of her usual behavior would have been refusing to shop for Mrs. Phipps and having nothing to do with Felix. But sudden changes were traumatic to old people. And she couldn't very well throw her own brother out on the street with the wolves and vultures of society waiting to tear him apart and pick his bones clean, could she?

No.

Still, the advice had worked twice and failed twice, in just one day. That was a 50 percent success rate. Even odds that, with time, she could turn her life around. And once Mrs. Phipps *gradually* grasped the idea that she wasn't a personal shopping service, the odds would get better. And Felix . . .

She opened the bathroom door and let the light shine into the room across the hall, where her brother lay sleeping in her bed. She had no idea of what to do about Felix. What did she know about loan sharks?

"You gonna stand there all night?" came his muffled voice. "That light's in my eyes."

"You shut up," she said, her lightweight anger coming in bursts between lapses of sympathy and concern. "Don't even talk to me. Not a word. I'm so mad at you, I could spit."

"Fine," he said, and she could hear him rolling over away from the light. "Elly?"

His voice sounded so young. Like a little boy's. Like her little brother's.

Her heart softened.

"What?"

"Be sure you lock the door when you leave."

It hardened again.

"What did I just tell you? I don't want to hear anything from you. Not another peep."

She waited a moment or two to make sure he got the message this time, then purposely left the door open when she returned to the bathroom to dry her hair. He needed a place to hide out for a while, he'd told her. Somewhere to gather his thoughts and decide on the best course of action. He hadn't asked her for money yet, and protecting him for a while didn't seem like too big a setback, considering he *was* her brother.

Question was, how to explain the debt-bedeviled drunk in your bed to your new date?

Dinner in Quincey—no matter which restaurant they went to—never required much dressing up. Sand-colored slacks and a white silk blouse were her first choice, the choice she would have normally made. She replaced them and, with a designing smile she didn't even know she owned, chose a low-cut spaghetti-strapped sheath she'd ordered from a catalog and never worn, instead.

She was dressed and finishing up her makeup—and getting a little nervous—when she heard a rap at her door. Strange how your hands can be so cold and your cheeks so hot when you have the jitters, she thought, placing one against the other to even them out. She left the bathroom mirror, checked herself in the hall mirror, then tidied herself at the door once more before opening it.

"Zowie! Will you look at you!"

"Oh. Hi, Eugene," she said, attempting a welcome smile for her neighbor and missing by a mile. Not that he noticed.

Bubba came to stand in the door beside her, took one look, then scurried down the stairs and out of sight.

Eugene occupied the other second-floor apartment. For the most part he was a quiet tenant who worked days in the local fan factory and spent much of his free time surfing the Internet in his darkened apartment. In the name of charity she tried not to liken him to a mole, but truth be told, he not only acted like one, he looked like one. Pinched face. Thick glasses. Dirty nails. Dark unkept fur . . . uh . . . hair.

"Looks like someone's got a date," he observed astutely. It might have been her nerves, but there was something about bugging eyes behind thick glass focused on her overexposed chest that made her want to scream and run.

"Someone does."

"Dinner?"

"Yes."

"No . . . leftovers, then?"

Oh yes. Along with his other rodentlike mannerisms, Eugene also scrounged for food. Too nice by nature, she'd found it extremely difficult to refuse him— despite the fact that accommodating him was extremely annoying and distasteful. His one saving grace was that he wasn't picky. He was delighted with the scraps in her frozen dinner trays; he thought a hastily made peanut butter sandwich and an apple a king's feast, and an unopened can of spaghetti set her up in his book of saints.

The mere mention of food was her cue to fetch him something to eat, but *if what you're doing isn't making you happy*—and it wasn't—*try doing the exact opposite.*

"No. No leftovers. None."

"None?" His gaze rose from her chest to meet hers.

"Nope. No leftovers tonight, Eugene. Sorry," she

added. She wasn't, of course. She felt liberated in an outlandish fashion. But old habits were *so* hard to break.

He shifted his weight from one foot to the other, his face twitching, sensing that something was wrong. When she didn't scoot off to find him something, his instinctive need to feed took him elsewhere.

"Want me to take your trash down for you?"

"What?" she asked, taken back. It wasn't an extraordinary question. He frequently took her trash down with his. It was a neighborly thing to do. Right?

"Your trash? Want me to take it down to the dumpster for you?"

"Ah. No." She motioned behind her with a finger. "Felix. He's here. He can take it down in the morning. But thanks."

"Felix?" He tried to look into her apartment. Clearly he hadn't seen the car parked on the front lawn as yet. "He's here? Is he your date?"

"No," she said, her voice taking an offensive tone. Her dates and her brother were none of his business.

"Isn't he going to eat?"

"No," she said, an octave higher. She didn't need to give him an explanation, she knew, but the insanity of the situation was getting to her. "He's . . . under the weather . . . a bit."

"Drunk," he said in a holier-than-thou tone she couldn't appreciate from a ratlike creature.

"Plastered," she said, picking her own adjective. "He couldn't eat with a feedbag tied to his face. But I appreciate your concern for him just the same."

Eugene frowned, stumped and hungry.

"Well, when he wakes up—"

"His head'll be bigger than his belly," she interjected. "He may not be able to eat for hours. Days maybe."

He was backing up to his apartment door. "Days . . . ?"

"And when he's feeling better, he'll be hungry as a one-man army and eat everything that isn't nailed down. He always does."

Plainly disgruntled, he retreated into his apartment and the door slowly swung closed. Ellen smiled. The little green book should have been printed in twenty-four-carat gold. Who knew it could be so easy to rid oneself of pesky pests, without actually being rude or unkind—or using a broom. She stepped back and closed her own door.

"You know," came a weak voice from down the hall, "I could eat something."

"Shut up, Felix. You can starve to death for all I care," she said. "And don't eat the leftover roast beef while I'm gone; I'm saving that for my lunches this week."

She cringed at the knock on the door. Eugene had heard "leftover roast beef" and had returned.

The grimace on her face slowly brightened to a dazzle as she took in Jonah Blake dressed in dark slacks and a sport jacket, the pressed white oxford shirt making the whites of his eyes whiter and the mystic green greener, though the light in them was no mystery at all. She didn't need to be someone with Vi's expertise to recognize the look in his eyes. She didn't need to be someone with an attitude or a little green book to know what he was thinking. She was born a woman and knew it instinctively.

She went warm and soft and gooey inside.

It pleased him, probably more than it should have,

to see that she'd gone to no little effort to dress up for their date. He'd been in Quincey long enough to know the dress code was casual, and had debated long and hard over his decision go one step further to impress her—now he was glad he had. Except . . . well . . . maybe he'd gone too far. She was staring at him. She was so beautiful and elegant . . . and so completely silent. His hand went to the open collar of his shirt self-consciously, and he fought an urge to squirm. He thought about buttoning it, then shoved his hand in his pocket.

"I decided to leave the cloak and dagger at home," he said, hoping she'd equate his lack of a tie with some sort of effort to fit into his present surroundings, rather than with his dislike of them.

"I'm glad," she said, aiming for a breezy attitude, her heart fluttering wildly. "You look very nice."

"You're beautiful."

A muffled groan from down the hall had him frowning. He pulled his gaze from hers and looked past her with some anxiety.

"Thank you," she said, reaching for the purse she'd set on a table near the door. "I'm also starving."

He looked confused and still concerned. "Didn't you hear that?"

"What?"

"That noise? Like moaning?"

"No." Amazing. With the proper attitude, lying was easy. She suspected that with an altogether different attitude, murder would be the same. "Ready?"

He nodded uncertainly, stepping aside to let her lock and close the door, then following her down the stairs. He wasn't one to hear things that weren't there or to forget small, inconsequential things readily. Details were his business, and as a rule, few escaped him. But her bare back and the sweep of her hair that left her throat exposed and vulnerable had a disturbing effect on his mind. Filled it, in fact, with nothing but thoughts of touching her, of pressing his lips to the warm nape of her neck, of drawing in the scent of her. . . .

"Any trouble getting here?" she asked, perturbed that Felix had dead-ended their discussion of her beauty—as if it were frequently debated, which it wasn't.

"No. None. In fact, I'd given myself a few extra minutes to get lost in, so I had to sit in the car for ten minutes before I could come up."

"Oh no," she said, glancing back at him, her stomach lurching with excitement when their eyes met. Breezy. Easygoing. Self-assured, she reminded herself. "You should have come up. Or are you a stickler for punctuality?"

"It's an old habit."

"Ah, yes," she said playfully. "A military-CIA-FBI-spy guy would have an old habit like that."

He chuckled as they came to the bottom of the stairs, and was about to reply when they heard Mrs. Phipps.

"Oh, Ellen," she said, swinging the door wide from its cracked position. "We thought we heard someone out here. We thought Eugene was bringing the trash down. But don't you look pretty," she added, looking at Jonah.

"Thank you. Mrs. Phipps, this is Jonah Blake. He's in town visiting his father for a while," she said, then addressed Jonah. "Mrs. Phipps taught third grade here for . . . how long, Mrs. Phipps? A hundred years?"

"Goodness. Was it only that long?" She laughed at

Ellen's gentle teasing. "Seems more like two hundred to us, although we have to admit it sometimes feels like it was at least that long ago since we did it. But then, time has a way of speeding up and slowing down all in the same day so you don't know how long ago anything has been." She held out her hand to Jonah. "And are you Earl Blake's son? From the camera shop downtown?"

"Yes, ma'am," he said, sliding his hand between both of hers, allowing her to rub and chafe it as they spoke. Ellen was relieved to see she wasn't the only one around with a soft spot for sweet little old ladies. "Do you know him?"

"Yes, indeed, though not very well at all. We understand he's ill. How is he?"

"He's had a stroke, ma'am. They say he's stable but . . ." He shrugged.

"Oh, what a shame, what a shame." She patted Jonah's hand sympathetically, then finally released it. "He is so talented. We remember him coming to our AARP meeting to talk about his pictures one time, years ago. He showed us the magazines and journals and told us about all the places he'd been to. He really is a fascinating man. You look a good bit like him, you know."

"I've heard that."

"It's true. And what do you do? Are you also a famous photographer?"

"No, ma'am." He and Ellen exchanged an amused glance. "I'm a terrible photographer. I haven't any artistic talents at all."

"What a shame. But then, neither do we." She laughed. "My son was very artistic though. Not like your father, but when he was little, he drew wonderful pictures in crayon. Very . . . alive. Colorful." She hesitated a moment as if she'd lost track of her thoughts. She did this sometimes—especially when she talked about her son, who had died in his adolescence in a farming accident. "And what is it you do?"

Again their gazes met and held and shared an amusement as Ellen turned toward him with great interest to hear his answer. Sharing a thought or idea with only a look, without touch or word or gesture, was very intimate somehow. An invisible linking between them. She liked it.

"Right now I'm trying to keep my father's camera shop afloat in case he recovers enough strength to go back to it," he said, evading the question not because he needed to, but to entertain Ellen. "From what I can tell, it's about all he's got, and he hasn't been able to tell me yet what he wants done with it. Leaving it closed up while I sat around the hospital doing nothing seemed like a waste."

"And it would have been. That's very good thinking, young man. We know your father will appreciate what you've done for him."

"I hope so."

"Oh, look at me. Holding you up in the hall here, all dressed up. You look so nice together. A very handsome couple."

They both smiled at her and edged toward the door, saying their good-byes and good nights.

"Nice lady," he commented moments later.

"Yes. Very nice."

"Nice night."

"Yes. Very."

"Nice parking job," he said, eyeing Felix's car.

She couldn't help it. She laughed, breaking the awkward what-to-talk-about-next tension between them. "I only know your father by sight," she said, watching as he opened the car door for her. "I didn't know he was famous."

"I didn't either." She looked startled, then confused, so he explained. "I mean, I didn't know the extent of his fame until I moved into his house here. I'd seen some of his pictures and knew he was well known, just not how well known."

"Oh."

He could see she was still bewildered as he swung the door closed and circled the car to get in on the other side. He wasn't used to having a father, much less talking about him, and the idea of discussing their relationship made him even more uncomfortable. Still, this woman was different; what he felt for her was different. Maybe he should treat her differently. Maybe he should make an effort to explain himself and his life to her. Open up a little. *Be* uncomfortable for a change, and not keep trying to avoid it.

He got into the car and fastened his seat belt, then turned toward her.

"I didn't grow up around my father. I hardly know him."

"Oh," she said sadly. "I'm sorry." She would have left it to his discretion to say more, if she were still too nice. However . . . "Were your parents divorced, then?"

"Yes," he said. Unable to simply sit and talk about it, he distracted himself by starting the car and pulling away from the curb. "He was gone before I was a year old. I didn't see him after that till I was six, when my mother died." He took a deep breath. "I can count on one hand the times I saw him after that."

Then who had raised him? Where had he grown

up? These questions kept her silent for a minute. She decided to take a giant leap forward and work her way back.

"Until now."

He nodded. "Until now. Now I see him every day, and we still don't speak to each other." He smiled at the irony.

"What sort of photographer was he?" she asked, fully aware that a great deal more had happened between them since he was six. She could hear it in his voice, tight and tempered. She'd blundered into an open wound and, too nice or not, couldn't bring herself to cause him any further pain. "Would I have seen any of his photographs?"

"Maybe. . . . There's only one Italian restaurant in town, on Glover; I checked. Is that where we're going?"

"Yes." He checked? Standard procedure for a mercenary-CIA-FBI-spy guy? What had she gotten herself into?

"If you've done much reading or research on the Vietnam War or the civil rights movement in the seventies, the riots and all," he was saying, turning into a busy intersection, "then you've no doubt seen several of his photographs. He has a wall full of photojournalism awards from the sixties and seventies and a couple from the early eighties. Forty of them maybe. Gruesome photographs. But you can tell he was good." He hesitated. "You can tell that he loved his work."

She mulled this over. "Is that when he moved to Quincey? When all the unrest died down?" Another thought. "Why Quincey?"

"I don't know for sure when he moved here," he said, sounding almost apologetic. "We'd lost all contact by then. The records on the shop only go back to 1990. He must have been doing something. . . ." His voice trailed off. "But I do know why he moved to Quincey," he said brightly, thinking it a real trick that he knew anything at all about him. "He inherited his house and the lease on the shop from a man named Levy Gunther. I found that out from his lawyer—who, by the way, didn't even know I existed. He didn't know the whole story either, but it seems this Levy Gunther was the father of some kid my father photographed and then later saved in a bombing or something. I guess this kid came home from Vietnam and eventually died of something else, leaving Gunther with no one to leave the shop to, so he left it to my father. As a sort of thankyou, I guess. And I suppose he thought someone like my father would appreciate a camera shop. So, according to the lawyer, my father showed up here about six years after the man died, and stayed. Paid the taxes. Painted the house. Opened the shop and settled in."

"Huh," she said, too wrapped up in the story to recall her attitude. "That's amazing. Did Gunther and your father ever actually meet?"

"I don't know," he said, stopping at a red light and glancing at her. The amazing thing was how easy she was to talk to. All he had to do was answer the questions she wasn't too shy or too apathetic to ask. She was genuinely interested in people—in him—and it showed.

"How old is your father?"

"Seventy-eight."

"Then he would have been about seventy when he came here." A pause. "I was just thinking that he should have opened a portrait studio or something here, so he could keep taking pictures, instead of just selling cameras. But maybe he was feeling too old for that. You know, I don't think I ever saw him out taking pictures around town. And I never heard talk about him being famous. Do you think he stopped taking pictures altogether when he came here?"

"I don't know," he said again, pulling into the parking lot beside Pappino's Italian Restaurant. When he'd parked and turned the engine off, he looked at her. There was such a sad expression on her face that he couldn't help asking, "Why? Why do you ask that? What are you thinking?"

"Just how hard it is to give up something you love like that. He wears glasses, I know. Maybe his eyes got so bad that he couldn't see well enough to take great shots anymore. That would be a horrible thing to have to admit to himself. Maybe he had nowhere else to go. Maybe he came here to sit out the rest of his life, waiting to die."

"Maybe," he said, and because his heart was overflowing with a venomous hatred and the air around him was heating with anger, he got out of the car. He stood there for a moment, gulping the cool evening air, trying to forget that his father had given him up long before he'd given up his beloved camera; that they both could have had a place to go in times of need if he'd been any kind of father to him.

It didn't help to remember. He sighed. It didn't help to remember because it wasn't enough to make him turn his back on the man now, when he wanted to most.

"Jonah?" He turned and looked at her over the roof of the car. "I'm sorry. I can see I've upset you. I didn't—"

"No," he said, shaking his head. "Not you. In fact, I'd appreciate it if you'd say more things like that." He laughed softly at how strange that sounded and walked around the car to her. "Say whatever comes to your mind. Say what you're thinking." He shook his head. "Because I don't know what to think. I don't know him, Ellen. He's my father and a complete stranger. Sometimes I hate him so much, I could kill him with his pillow. Sometimes I sit for hours staring at him, trying to see my face in his, to read his mind, to understand him. I don't even know where to begin." He took a step closer to her. Close enough to touch her. "What you said just now . . . about him giving up his photography and how it must have hurt him. I understand that. If it's true, I . . . I can't say I'm sorry, but it doesn't make me happy either." He studied her face for a moment. He found comfort in it, and the acceptance he needed to go on. "But it's something, one thing, that I can understand about him."

She didn't think about the inclination to reach out to him, to touch him. She just did it. Palming his cheek was the most natural thing to do, no matter what kind of person she was.

She didn't say anything. What was there to say? That he was hurting and confused was obvious. But they were both human, they both had feelings, and somewhere along the way their spirits had connected.

He stood perfectly still as long as he could, the warmth of her palm seeping through his skin, heating the chill that protected and preserved his heart. The lovely face he'd admired from afar was close enough to kiss, and the woman who owned it was more than he thought possible. In her eyes he could see the gentleness and perception he'd suspected her of having, but more, a true kindness and empathy that needed no words, no action to be activated. It was ever present in her, as spontaneous and unconscious as her next breath.

She felt his fist pressing softly below her chin, his thumb brushing along the curve of her lower lip. There was a tender gratitude in his eyes. And behind it, beyond the mysteries, was an all-consuming need that once unleashed would devour her completely. It frightened her and yet somehow she knew that he was . . . akin to the wind. That he could come at her hard and harsh, or slow and gentle, and the effect would be the same—she would be changed forever, reshaped, different. And like the wind, he would be unstoppable.

He tipped his head and leaned toward her, pressing his lips against hers, then hesitated. She knew the first kiss had been born of gratitude. She knew, too, that the second one wouldn't be. He was giving her a chance to run, to refuse him, to protect herself. But in that moment no little green book, no attitude, no promotion, no pay raise, no huge character flaw was more important to her than that next kiss. There was nothing left to the world but him and her and that kiss.

She put her lips to his, moved her hand from his cheek to the back of his head, where his hair was thick and soft in her fingers. She felt his hands at her waist and stepped closer, opened her mouth to the first tentative touch of his tongue and was instantly lost.

A dam of pent-up emotion broke free inside him. Mingled with the acute physical sensations and the thrilling excitement was an overwhelming stir of relief, and he wasn't sure why. Maybe it was simply good to confirm that she felt as right in his arms as he'd hoped. Perhaps it was just a matter of getting the first kiss out of the way. Or of knowing she hadn't been averse to a second. But it was such a huge relief, a relaxing sigh from his soul, that he believed it was something much more significant.

They came away breathless and feeling awkward, stared at each other in amazement. Then they laughed, their arms falling away to hang loose at their sides, their common sense forcing them to take mental steps backward.

Ellen scrambled immediately for her lost attitude. What would he think if she made too much of the kiss? That she'd never been kissed that way before? That she'd wanted him to kiss her that way? Well okay, she had, but . . . She was shaken to her very core and feeling vulnerable as hell. Attitude was the perfect shield to hide her fears and make her appear brave and strong—and kissed like that all the time.

Jonah, on the other hand, was much more adept at hiding his feelings and recovered much quicker.

"You should have been a shrink," he said casually, closing the car door and, with a light hand to her back, leading the way to the restaurant. "You're very easy to talk to."

"I get that a lot," she said lightly. "But if I hung out my shingle, talking would become my job and not as much fun. I'd have to charge people and get a fifty-minute watch. No, I think I'll stick with my amateur status. Then I only have to talk to people I want to talk to, and I can use my expert skills for other things." She arched a sly brow at him.

Looking duly cautious as he held the door for her, he asked, "Such as?"

"Such as extracting information from mysterious men who work in camera shops," she said, smiling mischievously as the hostess approached them.

Pretending enlightenment, he grinned at her. And

while her stomach embarked on an Olympic-style acrobatic routine, he turned the exact same grin on the hostess and asked for a table for two. Ellen sighed, disgruntled, and followed the woman toward their table.

Seated, menued, watered, and alone again, they simulated a detailed investigation of the meals available while their minds pondered their next moves and their hearts yearned to return to the parking lot. When their gazes met over the tops of their menus, they recognized themselves in the other's expression and smiled. They were the same really. Both nervous. Both attracted. Both wanting the night to go well so there could be others. Both needing. Both a little shy and reserved. Both remembering the kiss, and both a little overwhelmed by it all.

First dates were so tedious, she thought. Really. So regimented and traditional. Why should a passionate kiss in the parking lot less than twelve hours after they met throw the whole thing off? Or had it? Maybe their instincts knew best.

"Just don't tell me you're a mercenary, okay?" she said, forcing herself to break the silence first, using the playful, carefree attitude he seemed to like. "I'm not at all sure how I'll react to that."

He chuckled and grinned, laying his menu on the table, folding his hands on top.

"Okay," he said, simply enjoying the sight of her across the table from him. "I'm not a mercenary."

"Or a spy. You say it out loud and, date-wise, you think . . . unreliable." The twinkle in her eyes was humorous. "Like he'll go to make a phone call between dinner and dessert and disappear—leaving you with the bill and a long walk home."

Silent laughter.

"Spies have gotten a bad rap. Most of them live very normal, very ordinary lives."

With the humor fading quickly, she whispered, "You're a *spy*?"

She would have bet her last dime there wasn't one word of advice in the little green book that addressed the dating and charming of spies. And she *really* wanted to charm him.

"No. Not exactly."

"FBI?"

"Not exactly."

"CIA?"

"No. Not quite."

"Oh God." She moaned. "You're not one of those special forces guys they make the movies about who go off alone to do all the dangerous stuff no one else will do, are you?"

He laughed heartily this time. "You mean women aren't really attracted to the action-adventure types?"

"Well, in the movies, yeah. But in real life?" She looked mighty dubious.

Still amused, he said, "In real life I rarely go off anywhere anymore outside the United States, and what I do is probably less dangerous than what you do." He chuckled again. "But the truth is I'm a captain in the United States Navy, attached to the Naval Sector of DIAC in Washington, D.C. Most days I work nine to five in an office with no windows."

"The Navy? Really?"

"Disappointed?"

"No. Not at all," she said. "Relieved. And you live in Washington? Oh, that must be fascinating. So many things to see. The museums and the people and historic buildings and—have you seen the president? In person?"

"Several times," he said, highly entertained by her reaction. Pleased to have pleased her.

They ordered and their meal came while she rattled off the names of people he may or may not have seen or met, and asked him about the places he'd been to and things he'd done. She was making this getting-to-know-you period—this impossibly frustrating part of his relationships—so easy. Granted, he generally chose women who could care less about who he was or what he did, but there was a reason for that. He simply thought that no one really wanted to know. But Ellen did. She hung on his every word. She'd grow quiet and thoughtful, then ask questions. Correlated the answers into what it meant to him or for him and was genuinely interested. No little thing was too little for her; it all intrigued her. He couldn't recall the last time he'd intrigued anyone, and the revelation was heady.

"Now tell me about this place you talked about before. The one you're attached to?"

"DIAC," he said, watching her cut her veal Parmesan a little slower than she had at the beginning of the meal. She was getting full, he noticed, noting everything she did and the way she did it with an uncommon interest. With an uncommon satisfaction as well. "The Defense Intelligence Analysis Center. That's where I work, what I do."

Her eyes narrowed slightly in thought. "You . . . analyze intelligence?"

Oh man. He'd just finished explaining that the Senate and the Congress weren't located in the House of Representatives. He must be thinking she was the biggest nitwit to draw air.

"Not that kind of intelligence," he said as if he could read her mind, though he was simply reacting to the confusion he always got when he told civilians what he did. "Information. I analyze information from satellite photos, from sonar and radar readings. Surveillance reports. Ship logs. Debriefings. That sort of thing." She was staring at him. "It all comes to the Center. Information gathered by NASA, the FBI, the CIA, Naval Intelligence, allied foreign governments, the FCC . . . everywhere. Tons of raw data. We look at it, compare it to other things we know, feed it into computers, record it, dissect it, add to it, figure it out, decipher it. Then we put it all in a report and send it upstairs to the decision makers. My superior officer, the JCS—the Joint Chiefs of Staff—the Department of Defense, the president . . ."

"Spy stuff," she said, her voice breathy and awed.

He opened his mouth to deny it, but then reconsidered. "Yeah. I guess so. Spy stuff."

"You profile foreign officials and military leaders down to the toothpaste they use and the decisions they'll make in any given situation and . . . and you use those photographs to see if anyone's developing new kinds of airplanes and ships and bombs and things."

"That's right." So easy.

"Just like in the movies!" she said, and they both laughed.

"Tell me how you got into that," she said, developing a true fondness for the sound of his voice—strong and smooth, like aged brandy. "Did you always want to do that? Is it hard? Do you have to go to a special school or something? It must be really interesting."

So very easy.

Through the rest of the meal and over cappuccinos, he told her about the natural progression of his career. From Annapolis to submarines, from radio specialist to specializing in sonar and radar, from his promotion to Naval Intelligence to his present assignment at DIAC. She listened avidly, made him slow down or back up to ask questions, and, in general, made him feel like the most important man in the world.

She was like that, he knew. She listened to everyone. Made everyone feel important. Was nice to everyone. He'd watched through the bank window. He knew this. But it didn't matter. He had her undivided attention—and for however long he had it, there just didn't seem to be anything better.

Returning from the restroom, he found her deep in thought, and, in the candlelight, looking almost like something he'd conjured from a dream. All that burnt sienna hair, streaks of vermilion shining bright and healthy. Her eyes hidden by her lowered lids; lashes dark and thick, curved up against the smooth paleness of her skin. Her lips lush and full and soft-looking in their relaxed state; her neck long and elegant, implying innocence, but begging to be nuzzled.

He took a deep breath and let it out slowly for control, then sat down across from her again.

"You look so far away there," he said with a curious tilting of his head. "What are you thinking about?"

She gave him a calculated look. "You," she said.

"What about me?" There was a twisting, fluttery feeling in the pit of his stomach that he was beginning to anticipate and enjoy.

She considered him a minute, trying to decide if she should tell the truth about what she was thinking or come up with something else to keep him distracted.

The little green book didn't say she should *always* go in the opposite direction. Only when it suited her purpose, and this time it didn't.

She leaned toward him in earnest. "I was wondering if you'd had a chance to talk with anyone else in town? If you've told anyone else what you've told me tonight. About your job?"

He shook his head. "No. Not really. Between the hospital and the shop, I've been sticking pretty close to home. Why?"

"Not your father's lawyer? Or someone who's come into the shop? You haven't told anyone else in town about your job?"

"No," he said, at a loss. "No one. I—"

He was about to explain that he wasn't an extrovert, that he could talk to someone for hours and never mention anything personal if he wasn't in the mood to share—and he was rarely in the mood—but she smiled and shook her head. She didn't need an explanation. She already knew.

"I was just thinking that if you hadn't told anyone in town about your job before now, that it was sort of interesting how close all the speculation about you really was." He frowned. "The mercenary/war hero/CIA-FBI-spy guy that was either a loving son or nephew that no one seemed to know anything about." He started to laugh. "No. Think about it. It's like that gossip game that kids play where one whispers something into the next person's ear and he whispers into the next person's and so on down the line. And when the last person tells what he's heard, it's completely false or a garbled mess of the truth. You're not a mercenary or a war hero but you're in the military. You're not with the CIA or the FBI but you work with them, and where you work is referred to by its initials. You're not a spy, but you do spy work . . . sort of." She bobbed her head. "You're a relative—a son or a nephew."

For an intelligence analyst he didn't seem to be computing very quickly.

"Don't you see? You said you and your father had lost touch long ago, that you didn't even know where he was until after he'd had his stroke. But someone in this town knew all about you and told someone else, who told someone else, and that's how things got so confused but still held some element of the truth. And how did whoever it was that notified you, know where to reach you?"

His gaze slipped away from her face, roamed a bit, and then returned.

"You think my father kept tabs on me?"

"Who else?"

"And he might have told someone about me."

"I'd say he bragged about you." When his expression turned ambivalent, she hurried on to convince him. "Come on. Mercenary, war hero, CIA, FBI, spy? Those are all fascinating and heroic and dangerous. That's the truth and pride getting blown out of proportion on its way through the grapevine. If he'd never said anything about you, there wouldn't have been any rumors at all, or maybe just that you were his son, from your meeting with the lawyer. Or if he hadn't been proud or known exactly what you were doing all that time, he might have casually mentioned to someone that you were a sailor, and the rumor would have gone through the mill and come out that you were a bum from the docks somewhere."

"You're really reaching here," he said. "And I appreciate what you're trying to do and all . . ."

She could tell he didn't appreciate it at all. "I'm not doing anything but telling you what I really think. You said I should."

If she was right, and if for one second he started to believe she was right, a whole new bag of bugs would open up, and he wasn't sure he'd want to look into it. Still, there she was, her honesty and sincerity as plain in her expression as the pale scattering of freckles across the bridge of her nose. She was a thoughtful woman—he'd seen a hundred examples of it—and she was simply too nice, too kind to instill false hopes where they didn't belong.

"I did say you should. And I still want you to. I just can't promise I'll always agree with you."

CHAPTER FOUR

STEP FOUR

Say no . . . and mean it.
—Nora Roberts

Though it's easy to spell and one of the shortest words in the English language, no is extremely hard to say and even more difficult to enforce. But it's not impossible. No is a complete sentence in and of itself. No explanations are needed. No excuses required. If you mean to say no, say it. Then say it again. And again . . .

"No. No. No," she told her mother over the phone. "Do not touch your savings or even think of cashing in one of your bonds to pay his gambling debts, Mom. You need that money to live on." It was midmorning and already her stomach was growling for lunch. Hungry and now angry she could hear her own voice puncturing the ceiling of the requisite noise level inside the bank. She glanced about, saw heads turning, and lowered it. "Listen to me, Mom. Just giving him the money isn't going to help. He'll do it again and again until you're broke." She listened. "No, I can't get him a loan here. He has no collateral and I know he won't pay it back. No. No. I haven't abandoned him. I told him this morning I'd help him think of something, and I will. But you have to promise me not to give him another dime." She waited. "Promise me. Okay. Now try to relax. Remember your blood pressure. We'll think of something. I love you too."

She hung up the phone and pressed her eyes closed with her fingers. This lesson in saying no was getting a real workout. She'd told Felix, "No. No. No," earlier that morning when he'd suggested *she* loan him the money.

"I won't," she'd said, recalling that the counselor she and Jane and her mother had gone to see about Felix's drinking problem had said it would only make his drinking easier for him, loaning him money, solving his problems for him. "I couldn't anyway. I don't have that kind of money just sitting around."

"It doesn't have to be the whole ten thousand. Five would keep them off my back for a while," he said, nursing a cup of black coffee. He actually looked better drunk than sober these days. To see what he'd become was heart wrenching.

"You don't have anything you could sell? Nothing stashed away?"

He gave her a flat look. "You mean all the stale air she left me after the divorce? I doubt anyone would be interested in buying the air I breathe. But maybe this old shirt?" His expression brightened falsely. "Think I could sell the shirt off my back?"

"I'm trying to help you."

"Then you're going to have to come up with more than a buck fifty-two. These guys are serious, Ellen."

"I realize that," she said, getting up from the small kitchen table to put her cup in the sink. She hesitated and frowned over his reference to a buck fifty-two, then let it go. "I have to go to work. You stay here today. Sleep. Don't drink. Don't go out to drink. I need time to think."

"Don't take too long."

"Ellen?" She jumped at the sound of her name, turned to find Joleen standing beside her desk, looking concerned. "Is everything all right? Are you all right?"

"No," she said automatically. "But I will be. It's just some personal stuff. Can I do something for you?"

Joleen looked around them for privacy, then bent low and spoke in a soft voice. "It's about the loan you've applied for at Quincey's First Savings and Loan."

"What loan?"

She made an awkward noise in her throat. "The loan they called here to get a personal reference for just now. As an employee of First Federal, you should have come here first, dear. I know it isn't any of my business, but we have special rates for—"

"I haven't applied for a loan anywhere. I don't know what you're talking about, Joleen."

"You cosigned? On a loan application? Yesterday? With your brother?"

"No. No way. No. I didn't," she said, shaking her head as the pieces fell into place. "Yesterday. No. Joleen, I'm sorry," she said, reaching for the telephone. "For taking up your time. For taking up the Savings and Loan's time. I'll call them right now and straighten this out."

Joleen straightened up, completely dumbfounded. She lingered a moment, then wandered off.

Ellen was mortified, with a singular craving for blood with her lunch. After settling things with the Savings and Loan—a simple matter of canceling the request she hadn't made in the first place—she took a few minutes' refuge in the ladies' room, locking the door, checking both stalls, then sitting on the counter next to the sink to think of something pleasant . . . anything pleasant.

Naturally, Jonah came swiftly to mind, and she smiled. What a wonderfully strange creature he was. Quiet and reserved was her initial perception, but she hadn't factored in thoughtful and intelligent, really intelligent. A thinker. An observer.

She hadn't realized she was tired of sitting in one position over dinner until he'd suggested they leave—and yet the minute he did, she knew that something in her manner or posture had given her away. He was like that, watching her all the time. Not as if she were a bug under glass, but as if she were a creature he wanted to know in its natural habitat, because it mattered to him. Because he wanted it to survive and thrive in his presence, as if he were an intruder or a foreign organism in a pristine petri dish. Watching her to see if he could fit into her life somehow, without damaging it, without upsetting the natural balance of her existence.

The derisive noise she made echoed through the restroom. If he knew how unbalanced her life really was, he wouldn't look twice at her. Well, he might look, but he'd see she was just a too-nice person who couldn't stop people from walking all over her.

With more to say and so much more they wanted to know, they had both been reluctant to cut short their first date. It had been a perfect summer evening with a bright half-moon and more than enough stars in the clear night sky. They'd walked up one side of Glover Street and down the other, talking, talking, talking. They were so alone in their own little world, they didn't notice the change in their surroundings from commercial to residential until the streetlights grew few and far between and she tripped over a piece of uneven sidewalk.

"Oops. You okay?" he asked, still holding her, a protective arm wrapped behind her after successfully breaking her fall. "Maybe we shouldn't have come so far without infrared, for night vision."

She laughed and held on to him until she was steady . . . and for just a little longer after that.

"You mean you don't have any special equipment sewn into the lining of your jacket? Or folded into the heel of your shoe?"

"Sorry. Wrong guy. You're thinking of James Bond."

No, she wasn't. She was thinking that his arms felt good around her, strong and safe, and that she liked the way he smelled, soapy and male.

"Oh, that's right. No British accent. We're doomed."

"Not yet, we're not." With his arm still around her, he turned her back the way they'd come. "Here, lean on me. I have super X-ray vision."

"That's Superman."

"Oh yeah. Well, I'm surefooted. How's that?"

She chuckled and adjusted her rhythm of walking to his. "I think that was the last Mohican."

"How about we just stumble back together?"

"I like that one." She smiled at him.

"Me too," he said, his voice low and soft, the warm pleasure in it heating her blood. "Now, where were we? You have a mother and a married sister and they both live here in town and . . . oh yes, you were going to tell me about your brother."

"No, I wasn't." Not tonight. Not anytime soon if she could avoid it. "I was about to ask you a question."

"Ask away."

"Do you gamble at all?"

"Gamble. Do you mean with cards, or with life in general?"

Well, now that he made the distinction . . . "Both."

"No. I'm not much of a risk taker. Personally or professionally. A finely tuned calculation is about as close as I get to taking any kind of chance on something I don't know for a fact. Even when I act on instinct, I have facts to back it up. It's the nature of my job—my nature, too, I guess. As for gambling with cards . . ." He thought a moment. "We played a lot of poker when we were at sea. Hours and hours, as I recall. I wasn't very good at it."

"You lost a lot of money at it?" She heard the hopeful note in her voice and cringed.

"Probably," he said with a chuckle. "I never kept track. I'd lose what I had and quit. Play again after payday."

"But you didn't run up huge debts," she said. It was a statement more than a question, and while she was glad he was a practical sort of man, she also knew he wouldn't have the answer to Felix's dilemma and that she wouldn't feel comfortable discussing it with him.

He'd been glancing at her frequently, but now he

gave her a steady look. "Was your father a gambler? Did he have problems with it?"

"No. No. Nothing like that," she said, feeling bad about the gentle concern in his voice. He had problems of his own and didn't need to be concerned about hers as well. Besides, a not-too-nice woman with the right attitude could solve her own problems, right?

To ease his mind, she launched herself into the carefully constructed character study of her father she'd developed in her youth. The story of a family man who had worked every day as a foreman in a glass factory that was part of the huge Ball Corporation out of Muncie. The man who drove the family up Interstate 69 every summer, stopping in Marion to pick up cousins, depositing them all at the family-owned cabin on Salamonie Lake for the summer—returning to Quincey to spend the summer alone, to work. A Hoosier fan. A member of the American Legion. A sportsman who liked to hunt and fish. A man who led his life happily and contentedly.

And that was where her adult version of the story would have kicked in, had she allowed it. A man who led his life happily and contentedly—as long as he had a beer in his hand. Funny, he hadn't seemed like an alcoholic; she never thought of him as one. He wasn't like Felix. She'd never seen him falling-down drunk or abusive or in any way different than the fathers of all her friends—except that he liked to drink beer on hot afternoons, after work, after dinner, in the car, after church on Sundays, during the Hoosier games. . . . But by the time he died of liver disease six years earlier, Felix had long been showing signs of having serious problems. By the time they sought counseling for Felix's problem, it was too late to help her father and too late to remodel her memory of him.

Oh, in her mind she knew the truth, but what she told Jonah was the only truth her heart would accept.

"And were you Daddy's little girl?" he'd asked when she finished.

"His favorite, you mean?" He nodded and she laughed. "Oh, no, that was Felix. Felix was everyone's favorite. The baby. The only boy. Even Jane and I spoiled him rotten."

He smiled at that, looking thoughtful. "You never did tell me about him," he said. "What does he do? What's he like? Does he live here in town too?"

They had returned to Pappino's parking lot by then, and as he led her around the car to the passenger side and unlocked the door for her, she scrambled for the best honest answers.

"He does live here in town. He's divorced. Right now he's sort of at . . . loose ends, you know?"

He nodded his understanding. "I've seen what divorce can do to people."

She hated not telling Jonah the whole truth about her brother. She even had a feeling he would understand the disease and empathize with her and Felix both. It wouldn't change what was happening between them, she was sure of that. She just . . . simply . . . couldn't. Every time she was tempted to, something inside would cry out, "No. No. No."

A note of humor in her throat reverberated off the tiled walls in the ladies' room. It was a good thing she hadn't read Step 4 the night before. Not that she would have used it then. Not that she'd needed to when her mind, her heart, her body and soul were all screaming, "Yes! Yes! Yes!" when Jonah had put a hand on the wall behind her and leaned forward to kiss her good night at the door. Softly. Gently. Oh, so sweetly. She sighed. He was a wonderful kisser. Hot and passionate in the parking lot. Tender and sensuous at the front door. Another deep sigh.

"Thank you for taking a chance on a stranger," he'd said, a breath's distance from her lips. "I had a good time."

"Mmmm . . . me too," she said with her eyes closed, no feeling in her feet. "I'd love to do it again with a friend."

"What about tomorrow night?"

"Tomorrow night?"

They shared a long, hot, passionate kiss that almost melted her panty hose.

"Follow me home after work tomorrow night," he said, sounding urgent. "I'll cook."

"Okay."

He kissed her again as if he might not have another opportunity, then slowly backed away from her. "Tomorrow night, then."

She'd nodded dumbly as droplets of logic trickled into her brain. *You have the right to be happy. Know what you want. It's your destiny. Think about the choices you make. Turn left and go that way.* It was in her mouth and almost passed her lips to call him back, invite him upstairs, and keep him there forever.

Then she remembered Felix.

Even after she'd watched Jonah drive away, then floated up the stairs to her door—stepping sideways to impulsively drop her doggy bag of veal Parmesan outside Eugene's door—she was tempted to race down to the back of the house, get in her car, and follow him home right then. The yearning inside her was like a black hole in space, a gaping, bottomless void that closed when his arms curled around her and opened again when he moved away. What a wonderfully strange creature he was. . . .

But again she remembered Felix.

Her growl of frustration echoed through the restroom. Her escape was finished. She wouldn't be able to successfully get on with her life until Felix and his problems had been dealt with. And where the heck was she going to get ten thousand dollars without ruining her life or her mother's life or her sister's?

The last time they'd banded together to help Felix, they'd sought counseling. They'd been advised not to pay his debts, to let his credit rating drop into oblivion, and in general *let* him make his own life as miserable as possible. The counselor had said it would be Felix's own misery that would eventually compel him to seek help and turn his life around.

Unfortunately, there had been no advice on how to deal with loan sharks without losing limbs. She probably should have asked about it—Felix could be very charming and was good at borrowing things. But at the time, she hadn't even realized Quincey had shylocks, much less that her brother was gambling.

She picked up Mrs. Phipps's groceries at lunchtime and tried not to let her mind wander throughout the rest of the afternoon—but it wasn't easy. She vacillated between canceling her date with Jonah and going home to murder her brother, then trying to deal with his problems. But as murder was against the law, and since she had no real solution for Felix—and because she couldn't keep her eyes from gravitating toward the front window and the camera shop—that decision made itself.

And so, when at five forty-five her peripheral vision registered movement across the street, she glanced away from her computer and bit into her lower lip with excitement at the sight of him, tall and straight and broad shouldered, locking the shop door. Her blood pumped hard and fast and hot through her veins.

He turned, caught her watching him, and smiled. She frowned, squinted, and turned the corners of her mouth upward, venturing a guess at the significance of his smile. It was certainly a nice one, a wonderful smile that had her heart in her throat, but . . . Well, it was also a "Hi. I'm ready. How about you?" greeting-type smile that he might have given a coworker he planned to play baseball with.

There was a sagging, sinking feeling in her chest that made her restless and discontented. She *liked* Jonah. Better than she'd liked any man in . . . maybe ever, she guesstimated. Certainly no man had ever made her itch from the inside out the way he did. Or intrigued her as much. Or touched her so deeply in places she hadn't known existed inside her. None had lit such a fire in her belly to step up and be noticed by them, certainly, or to speak out or to assert herself in an active, calculated pursuit of *them*.

The soft laugh that escaped her came with self-awareness.

A significant smile meant just for her, her fanny! She wanted to bring him to his knees, to make him fall helplessly and hopelessly in love with her—the way she'd fallen for him. Thinking about it, her aberrant reaction to Vi's interest in him seemed very . . . berrant now. Natural and logical—or as natural and logical as jealousy could be, anyway.

Her resolve fortified itself as she cleared her desk and got ready to hurry out to the parking lot to meet him. She wasn't going to need Step 4 for the rest of this evening either, she thought, noting the little green book tucked inside her purse. Saying no to Jonah was not part of her plan.

"Hi," she greeted him moments later, sure that her expression was revealing her shiny new acumen. She was in love and she wanted the whole world to know. And Jonah, too, of course.

"Hi," he said, coming away from his leaning position on the hood of her car. "That gray dress is my favorite."

She laughed, a little giddy. Her dress was teal blue, but if he had called it yellow or cherry red, it wouldn't have made a bit of difference. Not with the way he was looking at her. "I'll wear it more often."

"I like the navy suit you wear with the bright scarf too."

"Then I'll alternate between the two and throw the rest of my clothes away," she said brightly, and they laughed. She felt another peculiar sensation stir inside her. She liked making him laugh, she *wanted* to please him.

They met beside her car, their hands and arms instantly tangling like four loose cords.

"Can I kiss you?" he asked abruptly. He had no qualms of his own, but he didn't want to cross any invisible lines she might have about public displays of affection. If he didn't kiss her soon, he knew he'd implode—but he'd rather do that than cause her uneasiness. God knew, he was uneasy enough for both of them. He felt as if he were living inside a tornado, his thoughts whirling, his emotions sweeping and powerful, his body in knots. "Now? Here?"

"I really wish you would," she said, stepping closer to him, lifting her face to his. "Right here. Right now."

It was like eating chocolate cake. A small tentative taste, then a chocoholic pig-out.

With his hands at her waist he held her away and sighed, temporarily restored.

"Ready?" he asked, feeling even more nervous than he had the night before—if that was possible. The previous night she'd taken a gamble on him and had broken even. Tonight he wanted to make her feel like a winner. And tomorrow? Well, tomorrow he'd convince her that he was the lucky charm she couldn't live without. He had it all planned. He'd take it slow, one step at a time. He didn't want to screw anything up. He wanted everything to be perfect.

If she were just some woman, it wouldn't matter, but everything about this woman mattered. He didn't want to be too cavalier or cling too tight. Didn't want to be too pushy or too big a pushover. Didn't want her to think he was trying too hard or not trying hard enough to make her happy. And when they came together, when they made love . . . he didn't want to jump her bones in a parking lot. He wanted it to be the right time, the right place. Prolonged and glorious. He wanted it to be as perfect as she was.

When she nodded and moved to unlock her car door, he crossed the lot to his car and got in. He'd opened the shop late that day, taking time at home to stock groceries, chill wine, and straighten up the house. He'd even changed the sheets on the bed—just in case. But looking back on it, it surprised him how low on the list that task had been. Oh, he wanted her. No doubt about that, but somehow it seemed sort of secondary to simply spending time with her. He laughed out loud. *Secondary*, wasn't the right word. He wanted to crawl inside her skin and make it his own. He wanted to possess her body and soul, to hear her moan with pleasure, cry out in surrender. Still, holding her hand during a movie or linking arms with her when they walked together, sharing tidbits of news with her over morning coffee tempted him with a different, but equal force. He needed to be with her.

You could hit all the stoplights and still make it from one end of Quincey to the other in fifteen minutes. So it wasn't long before they lined their cars up at the curb in front of the house Earl Blake had inherited from Levy Gunther. A tidy little box-shaped place with white siding, black shutters, and outrageous crops of red impatiens spilling from window boxes on either side of the front porch; thick and bushlike along the walk. And recently trimmed, Ellen noticed, as she followed Jonah up the front steps.

It spoke volumes about the kind of person he was that he'd not only moved into his father's house and kept his father's shop open, but trimmed his flower beds and in essence maintained the man's life while he wasn't able to—in spite of the fact that he barely knew him and harbored no little bitterness toward him.

"What can I do to help?" she asked a short time later. He had immediately offered her a variety of drinks—from which she'd chosen a glass of white wine—and asked her to make herself comfortable. But she couldn't just stand around the neat little kitchen watching him do all the work. Not that he didn't look perfectly capable of it. "You know, I don't think a man's ever cooked for me before."

"I'm the first?"

"You're the first."

"Well, I don't know if throwing slabs of meat on the barbecue is really cooking," he said, looking up from his slicing and dicing of the salad parts. "But I'm trying to impress you here, so we'll go with that." He motioned to the counter in front of him. "And the mangling of vegetables, of course."

There was no mistaking his eagerness to dazzle her. The table set for two with candles and flowers was endearing. His frequent glances at the level of the wine in her glass and his constant awareness of her position in the room were heartbreakingly sweet.

She took a sudden left turn and went that way.

"Jonah," she said impulsively.

"Yes." He stopped everything to answer her.

With two and a half steps and all the courage she could muster, she wedged herself between him and the counter and said, "I'm already impressed."

No words could describe the subtle change in his expression that spoke directly to her heart, that seemed to welcome her home and promise an exciting adventure at once. His gaze, tender and wondrous, roamed slowly over her hair to her lips, across her cheeks and chin, deep into her eyes, and around inside her soul, claiming it all as his own.

"So am I," he whispered before he covered her mouth with his, the knife clanking on the countertop behind her before she felt his arms wrapping her slowly, surely in his embrace.

Life was so easy when you knew all the right steps to get you through it.

Reaching out for the stars wasn't necessary—not when everything she wanted was right here on earth. Reaching out and taking what she wanted was what life was all about. Reaching out, she looped both arms about his neck, took him into her heart, and sighed her satisfaction in knowing that with a little resolve, a little courage, and a little green book, she could have life *her* way. With that knowledge and Jonah's arms around her, there was nothing she couldn't do, nothing more she wanted.

Reach for the stars indeed. Funny how small the universe became when the love inside you was so vast. Aside from the scent of him, the taste and texture of his skin, the pressure of his arms and his hands gliding over the curves of her body, and the unbelievably spectacular explosions of sensations inside her head . . . well, the rest of the cosmos seemed to shrink to the size of a pinhead.

She was the surest thing in his life. He'd never known anything like her. Truly. Never. He could barely recall his mother, hardly knew his father, had never had a home. He'd always classified himself as a moderately ambitious man, because while he'd possessed the drive to achieve, he'd found it difficult to be absolutely certain of his decisions—not in his mind, but in his heart. The facts were always straight. The risk factors were always shaved down to a thread. Still, in his heart he was always afraid he'd walk straight into a pit of quicksand and be swallowed up whole. Until now . . .

He lifted his face from hers just to look at her again. Her eyes opened slowly, dazed and dreamy. Her lips were moist and rosy from his kisses. Her breathing was erratic. The pulse in her throat jumped wildly. He smiled and kissed her again to keep her that way. She'd stepped into that pocket of uncertainty inside him and filled it completely. Like a ball and socket or an elusive puzzle piece he'd been searching for all his life . . . There was still so much he wanted to know about her, but nothing more he *needed* to know. For the first time in his life he was absolutely, unequivocally, unconditionally, without reservation sure of something—her, and his love for her.

"Jonah," she murmured from a foggy place somewhere between heaven and earth.

The amazement in her voice amused him. "I know," he said, smiling, propping his arms against the counter behind her to hold the better part his weight as he leaned in for another quick kiss. She was so beautiful. "I know. I always thought I could almost imagine what this might feel like—but it's so much better."

They laughed and embraced each other again. It was still too new and too scary to say the words out loud, so they held each other, testing the reality of it.

"I didn't know," she said, her eyes closing as she listened to the steady rhythm of his heart through his chest. "I had no idea. And it happened so fast."

"Fast?" he asked, chuckling as he held her away from him. "I'm thirty-one years old. The last four weeks have been the longest month of my life. If you knew how often—" He stopped short when the phone rang. "Don't move."

"Yes, it is," she heard him say into the phone as he smiled at her across the kitchen. He frowned and turned slightly to the wall. "No, I hadn't planned on it tonight. I . . . is he . . . has something happened?" A pause. "Oh. Well, can it wait till morning?"

She began to shake her head decisively, long before

she whispered his name. "Jonah. No. We'll go tonight. We'll go now."

He shook his head and she nodded hers—they were both frowning.

"Okay," he said finally, to both her and the person on the line. "I'll be over shortly." He hung up the phone and turned to her. "Paperwork."

"Important paperwork or they wouldn't have called. They were expecting you. You visit with him every night, right? Tonight shouldn't be any different."

He didn't like the idea of giving up any part of their evening together, and it showed in his expression. "What about dinner?"

"Put it in the fridge. Some things keep, some things don't."

Part of him could easily liken his father to a slab of meat or a vegetable that would keep as well as their dinner, but it wasn't a part of himself he was proud of, or one he wanted her to see.

"You don't have to go too. You can wait here if you want. It won't take long."

"I'd like to go," she said. "If you wouldn't mind."

His arms swung out from his sides. "Why would I mind? I'd actually love the company. It's just not what I had planned."

She grinned at him. "According to Mrs. Phipps," she said, turning to inspect a bowl of fresh fruit for something that would sustain her till dinner, "behind every failed plan, a better opportunity is just waiting to happen. Orange or apple?"

"Apple," he said, coming up behind her. "An opportunity for something better or a better opportunity to do what you were planning to do in the first place?"

"Well," she said airily, handing him a shiny red apple and taking an orange for herself. "You just never know. According to Mrs. Phipps, that's the exciting part." Her eyes were bright with a suggestive sparkle. "You know, the part that makes life exciting?"

With serious eyes he studied her face even as his lips curved in amusement. Frankly, if you could measure excitement the way you could steam, he was about to pop. She made no secret of the fact that she wanted him, and the knowledge was twisting him inside out. He could barely breathe.

What amused him was her innocence, her incredible ignorance. He was delighted with it. She may have had sex before, may have wanted someone, needed them, but she'd never been made love to, never surrendered herself, never felt her world shatter, or she wouldn't be curling a come-here finger at a hungry wolf the way she was now. Teasing him and making silent promises were all well and fine, but if she were a wise woman—and he was glad she wasn't yet—she'd also be a little bit anxious, a tiny bit fearful, and much more impatient.

Perhaps, because he loved her, he should take this better opportunity to prepare her for what was to come.

In one sudden movement he pulled her up tight against him, covering her mouth with his before she could catch her breath. With passion hotter than the flames of hell, with skills devised by the devil himself, he bartered pleasure for her soul. He tempted and tantalized. Savored and satisfied. She moaned in bewildered abandon, and he smiled in his heart. She wasn't sure what was happening to her, couldn't fight it—liked it a lot. He felt her go limp in his arms as she gave in to it, tremble when it consumed her. It was eating away at his own senses, wearing him down, gnawing at his control.

Ellen stood there, stupid and staring, when he stepped away from her. For a second or two she thought the house had fallen on her, that she'd died and didn't know it yet. She felt nothing and then slowly, in the pit of her stomach, something alive and ravenous began to unfurl, growing and spreading, absorbing her, making her quicken and hunger for . . . for whatever it needed to live. It frightened her and at the same time she was captivated, taken by it, wanted more of it.

"Mrs. Phipps was right," he said, his voice a little thick. "Life is more exciting when a plan fails and a better opportunity comes along."

"Mmm," she said, nodding once in agreement, staring at him.

"You ready to go meet my father?"

She nodded again, and he smiled, taking great jubilation in her wary expression.

CHAPTER FIVE

STEP FIVE

A problem well stated is a problem half solved.
—*Charles Kettering*

It pays to be blunt sometimes. The shortest distance between two points is a straight line. There are people on this planet who don't understand anything but short, blunt, straight lines. So give them one. Be explicit. Be straightforward. You'll get to where you're going much faster.

"My fingers are sticky with orange juice," she told him. They were waiting at the nurses' station for the papers he needed to sign, before they went in to see his father. She did need to wash her hands, but more, she needed a few minutes to collect herself. They'd driven the short six blocks to the hospital. The air in the car had been thick with unspoken words, unfulfilled needs, and the low rumbling of things to come—like distant thunder before a storm. It made her tense and uneasy in a way that no attitude could hide. All she could think about was ripping his clothes off—touching him, feeling his skin against hers, tasting him, taking him inside her. Standing beside him at the nurses' station made her jumpy as a bee with six sore feet. "I'm going to find a ladies' room and wash up. I'll meet you at your father's room, okay?"

"Okay," he said, pointing down the hall in the direction of the nearest lavatory.

Knowing that he was watching her walk away, imagining what he might be thinking, made her knees wobble like a newborn calf's. What was happening to her? She took deep breaths and patted her face with cool water. Shook her hands and arms until there was no sensation in them at all. And all the while visions of Jonah danced through her head. Jonah laughing. Jonah talking. Jonah worried. Jonah sad. He was on her mind like moss on a rock . . . and she couldn't remember being happier.

When she entered his father's hospital room a few minutes later, she found Jonah sitting in a chair against the wall two or three feet from the foot of the bed. She smiled at him and he smiled back. With a small wave of his hand he silently introduced her to the thin, pale, gray-haired man in the bed.

Earl Blake had never been a large man. In his prime he would have stood four inches shorter than his son's six-foot-two-inch frame. Though they were both built wide in the shoulders and muscular, the term "thin and wiry" would have applied to Earl more than Jonah. Their eyes, however, were the exact same green, and where Jonah's seemed to contain the mysteries of life through the ages, Earl's were aged and held no life.

His head was elevated and he was propped to one

side with pillows, the sheets tucked in neatly, not a wrinkle in sight. That he didn't move much on his own was obvious. So was the extent of his paralysis.

She noticed homegrown flowers in plain glasses and canning jars placed about the room. While her heart twisted with Jonah's pain, it also ached with pride for loving such a sweet, giving man, as her gaze finally came to rest on him. He was sitting there, leaning on his arms with his hands clasped between his knees.

"Mr. Blake," she said, approaching the bed, coming to stand in what she hoped was his field of vision, though his eyes didn't move or register her presence. "My name is Ellen Webster. You might not recognize me, but I've been to your shop a couple of times to have film developed. I work across the street in the bank. Right there in the window." She paused, smiling, to give him a moment to recollect. "We've passed each other a hundred times in the street, but we've never actually met, I guess. It's funny, isn't it, the way you can think you know someone just because they're familiar, because you see them all the time? You know their name maybe and what they do, but you've never actually met?" His aphasia kept him silent, but she sensed he would agree with her. "Everyone at the bank was sorry to hear you were ill." She laughed a little. "Then Jonah showed up and you wouldn't believe the stir that caused." She laughed again and glanced over her shoulder at Jonah—who was staring at her, expressionless. She turned. "What? Did you think no one in the bank noticed when you opened up the camera shop again?" He started to shake his head. "Haven't you ever noticed how many women work in banks? Women notice men like you. Especially . . ."

"What are you doing?" he asked, cutting her off

rather rudely, though he wasn't as annoyed as he was surprised by her insensitivity. "He can't talk. He's had a stroke. He's . . . his mind is all . . ." He jumbled his fingers to illustrate. "He's in a coma."

"His eyes are open."

"They're always open. The nurses put drops in them during the day to keep them from drying out and at night they close them for him. He's . . . a breathing vegetable."

Frowning now, she looked at Earl and then back to Jonah. "The doctor told you that?"

"He didn't have to. Look at him. He can't see, or hear, or move anything."

"That doesn't mean he's not in there, Jonah. Just because he can't speak doesn't mean he can't hear, and just because he can't blink doesn't mean he can't see. He's not dead. He might still be in there somewhere. Thinking clearly. Hearing us . . ." This reminder caused her to move away from the bed and come to stand beside him.

Again he was shaking his head. "The doctor said the stoke was extensive, that there'd be permanent brain damage if he survived by some miracle. I know . . . I know what people say about talking to people in his condition, but . . ."

"But you're unwilling to try it?" She didn't mean to sound disappointed or disapproving, but she did. "It's not worth a try?"

"I don't think it would do any good." He sat up a little straighter, as if visibly putting up a defense shield to protect himself from her reproach.

"Do him any good or you any good?" she asked quietly with an inkling of understanding.

He looked at her for a long minute, considering,

then looked away. Did she somehow know that he came there every night wanting to tell him off, chew him out, send him to hell—but never did, because there would be no response, no expression of shame, no remorse? And so the anger remained inside him, festering and impotent, against someone so frail and feeble that to even contemplate hostile thoughts against him felt like . . . like kicking a dying dog.

"You know," she said quietly and thoughtfully, walking to the window and blindly looking out, "if his mind is still functioning, he knows you're here, and he's expecting you to be angry with him. It might be kinder, more respectful even, to give the strength of his spirit the benefit of the doubt rather than assume that his body is a hollow shell. He might *feel* more your equal if you treated him as if he were." She hesitated. "On the other hand, if he's not there anymore, then nothing you get off your chest is really going to do him any harm at all, will it?"

She turned then. He was watching her, taking in what she said, churning it around in his mind. Finally he shrugged and shook his head. The desire was there; he simply didn't know how to cross the river without a boat or a bridge in sight. Sometimes you simply had to jump in and start swimming. . . .

Ellen closed the short distance between them and held out her hand to him, saying, "Come on. Give it a try."

Closing his hand around hers, he let her lead him to the side of the bed. If Earl saw them coming, he didn't blink or twitch a muscle to acknowledge them.

"Mr. Blake," she said gently, "Jonah's been waiting a long time to talk to you. He knows you can't answer him and it's okay, so don't even try. He needs to say a few things." She turned her head to look at Jonah, whose expression was blank as he stared down at the man in the bed. "You have to start somewhere. Say the first thing that comes to your mind."

"He's an ass."

She smiled. Well, that was short and sweet and to the point—and it was a start. "Tell him."

"You're an ass." The sound of his own voice seemed to shake something loose inside him. It was as harsh and angry as his words. Together, they felt great. A long moment passed before another single thought entered his mind. "You shouldn't have left me the way you did." A little more plaster fell from the wall of anger he'd constructed inside himself. Ellen's hand was warm and steadfast in his, encouraging him to go on. "I was a little kid. I waited for years for you to come and get me."

It wasn't so bad. He wasn't being cruel, he was simply stating the facts as he knew them. Chances were, if the old man was well and able to speak, he wouldn't have had anything to say for himself anyway.

"I can see now, as an adult, that you couldn't have had a little kid tagging along on your photo shoots," he said reluctantly. "But you could have written once in a while. You could have called. We could have spent a few holidays together."

He felt Ellen move beside him and lost his train of thought. She was pulling the other chair closer to the bed for him.

"You're doing fine," she said, lowering him into the chair with her hands on his shoulders. "Sit down here and tell him what it was like. Tell him what you were like and what he missed. Go ahead."

He could hear her settling into the chair he'd vacated at the foot of the bed. He felt alone and awkward. Part of him felt like a fool talking to the unresponsive stranger in the bed, and yet he couldn't deny that with each secret pain he spoke aloud, with every repressed grievance he liberated, there came a certain lightness in his chest, an easing of the tightness he was accustomed to.

"I hated that school you sent me to," he said experimentally, feeling the release of another tight band from around his heart. "At first, anyway." A pause. "Like I said, I waited a long time for you to come get me. After a while I figured that school was the only family I was ever going to have. I had to make the best of it." He leaned back in the chair and laced his fingers over his abdomen comfortably. "Just for the record, though, you don't send a six-year-old off to military school unless there's something really . . . wrong with him, you know? Most of the kids in my class were hyperactive or had a discipline problem, along with feeling unwanted, so they ended up being weirder than I was." He was silent a moment. "But I actually think we all should have been at home at that age. Most of them went home for vacations. I dreaded vacations. Sometimes there were a couple of other guys who didn't go home, but usually it was just me, especially in the summer." He wasn't even thinking of what he wanted to say anymore. The words were out of his mouth without stopping in his brain for conscious thought. He was remembering, as if he were an outsider looking in, with no real feeling. "I suppose you made arrangements or at least knew I spent holidays and vacations with the commandant. He and I never had much trouble, we . . . we just stayed out of each other's way, ate meals together. The rest of time I was on my own."

Ellen listened as Jonah told his father about a young boy given light chores and class assignments during his vacations—idle hands and minds being what the were—and how he'd spent the rest of those idle hours of his youth shooting hoops and reading and repeatedly beating his own records on the two-mile track. He talked fondly about a camping trip with the campus cook and her family one Fourth of July, and Ellen could feel a resentment all her own building up against the pale, fragile man laying under the pristine sheets. It was impossible to remain objective, to try to see both sides. Because she loved him so much, it was too easy to see Jonah as a young boy, dark hair, big sober green eyes, alone and lonely. . . . She closed her eyes tight and held a deep breath. Her father may have been an alcoholic, but at least he'd been there, at least she knew he loved her. She let the sigh out and opened her eyes, stood and walked silently to the window.

There was nothing to look at really, nothing to distract her. It was dark out. From the second floor of the small two-story hospital she could make out several rows of streetlights in different directions and the emergency room entrance directly below and the parking lot beyond that. All was quiet, except for Jonah's deep, soft voice telling about a science fair he'd once won and how the commandant had told him his father would have been proud when he shook his hand and gave him the award. It had fired up a hope in his heart that his father was at least getting—and hopefully reading—reports about him. It spurred him to excel in everything. At his studies. In sports. To attain rank and privilege through the military system of the school. To make his father proud. To make his father want him . . .

She'd always known there were lots of people worse off in life than she was, and yet she still had the incredible nerve to complain about her lot, to feel restless, to want more. So much so that she'd turned to a ridiculous little green book for help. She knew a deep-down shame that made her want to cry. So she got tromped on a little, being a too-nice person, was that so bad? Maybe she didn't stand out in a crowd, was that so awful? What if she didn't have everything she wanted out of life, who did? And yet . . .

She'd almost convinced herself that it was okay to want to better oneself and to get more out of life, no matter how well off you'd always been, when she finally noticed what was happening in the parking lot below. Then she was certain of it. It was human nature to want more. It was her right to be happy—and to do what she had to do to make herself that way. Jonah didn't settle for being lonely and unhappy; she didn't have to either.

Watching from Earl Blake's sickroom, she let the scene below fuel her resolve. A police car had pulled up in front of the emergency room. Two nurses appeared from inside. She recognized Bobby Ingles as one of the officers—they'd gone to school together. His partner opened the rear door of their vehicle, and two long legs popped out. Kicking and flailing in the air, the legs were fast and agile, and looked as if they could cause some serious pain if they came in contact with someone. Bobby braved the leg farthest from the door and got kicked in the shoulder by the other leg for his efforts. His partner confronted that leg, wrapping both his arms around it the way he might a greased pig. They pulled together and eased the man out of the car. The two nurses were there, reaching to take first one arm, then the other with no problem at all. The man's hands were cuffed behind him.

They carried him like a battering ram, the two officers at his legs, the nurses by his arms, pulling him well away from the car, protecting him as he jerked and bucked, trying to free himself. Finally, when he either tired or decided it was useless, his neck went limp and his head lolled back so that he was staring straight up at Ellen in the second-floor window.

She wasn't sure if it was curiosity or disbelief that had her hyperextending her neck in an effort to get a good look at the man's face. She already knew who it was—and she was going to kill him.

She turned and through a haze of red she saw father and son circled in the light from the lamp above the bed. Jonah was leaning forward with his arms across his knees, speaking in a low voice. And with Earl positioned the way he was, she could almost imagine him listening.

It wasn't easy talking to the inanimate man, she could tell. Jonah would look at his hands, think of something to say, say it, wait for an answer, look back at his hands, and think of something else to comment on. She smiled. He was trying so hard. A part of him was still the little boy wanting love and acceptance from a man he barely knew, loving him instinctively, against his better judgment. It was a torment and a privilege to see, hurtful and uplifting at once.

She sighed. Perhaps not all of life was what you made it. Maybe it was a fifty-fifty combination of fate and free will. Thinking about it now, it seemed pretty fortuitous that she'd happened across the little green book when she had. Shortly after Jonah's arrival, after he'd caught her attention, just when she wanted to catch his attention. Maybe it was fate's way of saying that with a little self-improvement, she could be good for Jonah—that they could be good for each other.

But then, of course, there was the fact that the little green book was having no effect on her dealings with Felix.

"I'll probably never understand why you couldn't have kept in touch," she heard Jonah say. "Or forgive you. But I've seen your pictures."

"Jonah?" she said softly, hating to interrupt when he seemed to be on a roll. When he looked in her direction, she smiled. "I'm going to leave for a few minutes, a little while maybe."

"I'm sorry," he said, getting up immediately. "Of course, you're bored. I'm sorry. Let's go. This isn't doing any good anyway."

"No. No. It is," she said, rushing forward to keep him from moving the chair back "It is doing good. I can feel it." She patted her chest to show where. "And I'm not at all bored. I don't even want to leave, but . . . well, I just remembered a phone call I have to make. To my mother? I promised her I'd call her before nine, and here it is already eight thirty-five. But when she gets going . . ." She trailed off with a helpless laugh. Her face was hot. The next time she went to the grocery store, she was going to look for a little book titled *Lying Made Easy*. "It shouldn't take long, but it might be a while." She bobbed her head uncertainly. "I'll just go find a phone and call her and come right back. You stay. Keep talking to him. Tell him what you're doing now. I didn't bring my purse. Do you have a quarter?" If worst came to worst, she really was going to call her mother. "Tell him everything he's missed out on."

Uncertain, he handed her the quarter and said, "But

if we leave now, you can call from my house while I finish cooking dinner. We can make it back before nine."

Oh, she hated the perfect logic of that idea.

"You know, I was just thinking about that orange? I don't think it settled on my empty stomach very well. I feel sort of weird right now. I know it's rude and ungrateful to ask, but would you mind if we postponed dinner for another night? Maybe stop and get something light and fast after visiting hours?"

"Of course not," he said. A light chuckle mixed with a look of concern. "But how weird do you feel? Are you sick? You look a little pale."

"Me? No, it's the red hair. I always look pale."

"No," he said, leaning forward with a gentle kiss. "You always look beautiful."

"No," she said, embarrassed and a little flustered—and glad nonetheless that he kept coming back to that subject. "Well, sometimes maybe—but you should see me in the morning."

"I'd love to see you in the morning," he said quietly and quite seriously even as a wily smile played on his lips.

Oh Lord! Now she really was hot, and not just in her face. She felt her heart in her throat; it was beating too fast. This was one of those moments when a woman with a *real* attitude would say something hysterically funny to defuse the situation, or something so incredibly sexy, he'd forget to swallow his own drool. As it was, her mind was fizzling like a sparkler on Chinese New Year. He was looking at her as if . . . well, his whole expression was totally indecent considering where they were, with pain and suffering—and beds—all around them.

Her mind tipped slightly into hysteria. Tongue-tied, she sputtered a bit and shook her finger at him. All she could think about was waking up beside him, not caring what she looked like, knowing only that she was warm and safe and wanted. Finally she said, "I gotta go."

Once she made it to the first floor and followed the signs to the emergency room, it wasn't at all difficult to find Felix.

"Arrest me!"

She heard his voice the second she opened the doors to the waiting room.

"Arrest me! It's your job."

She approached the receptionist's desk and must have looked angry enough, or shamed enough, or determined enough, or enough like Felix for the woman to recognize who she might be. They exchanged embarrassed and empathic grimaces and the woman nodded and pointed, giving her silent permission to go through the doors leading to the emergency room.

"What kind of policemanship is this anyway?" she heard Felix ask, loud and indignant. "If you don't arrest me, I'll sue. I'll sue you. I'll sue the police station. I'll sue . . . my nose itches. Untie me so I can scratch it, okay?"

She didn't really want to be there, she realized suddenly. She was walking down the hall, looking into each treatment room, homing in on Felix's voice, but what she wanted to do was turn around, walk out, go home, crawl into bed, and forget about him.

"It's your duty to arrest me, Bobby. I'm drunk and disorderly, and I bet I broke something when I hit my head. That's . . . destruction. Destruction of property. You gotta arrest me."

"You didn't break anything. Nobody's pressing any charges. We'll call your mom or one of your sisters and have them come get you."

"My sisters," he said with some derision. "They're gonna love this. Hey! You were sweet on my sister Ellen in high school, weren't ya? I remember now." A brief silence. "Listen, if you ever had one ounce of feeling for her, you'd arrest me now. She *hates* funerals."

She stood outside the door with her back plastered to the wall, cringing with humiliation and remembering Bobby Ingles in high school—tall, skinny, and so shy he could barely string two coherent words together. Being what she was at the time, she had invited *him* to the movies after his tenth failed attempt to ask her out. He'd actually been a tolerable movie companion. He didn't utter a single word during the movie—or before or after it either.

"High school was a long time ago, and there isn't going to be any funeral," Bobby said. "You have a lump on your head, but the doc says you're going to be fine. He also says you need a detox program."

"What I need is to be arrested!" Felix bellowed.

"Felix!" she said, when she couldn't stand it any longer and stepped into the room. "Keep your voice down. There are sick people here."

"Now you've done it," he said to Bobby, casting him a traitor's glare. "If that junkyard dog doesn't kill me, she will."

"I'd like to right now. Hi, Bobby," she said, with a quick glance in his direction. Then she was back on Felix like white on rice. "I thought I told you to stay in my apartment and not to drink."

"You also told me you were going to fix things."

"And I will. As soon as I figure out how. In the meantime, you have to keep a clear head and stay out of sight."

"I think better drunk and I'll be safer in jail." He nodded his head to give her some assurance. He turned suddenly to Bobby and shouted, "Arrest me!"

She stepped back helplessly and saw for the first time that he had soft restraints around his wrists, tied to either side of the stretcher. He was wearing the same dirty clothes he'd been wearing the day before, which meant he hadn't even gone home to change before going out to drink—but then, why would he?

"I'm sorry about this, Bobby," she said when she looked up and caught him looking at her with a sad expression on his face. "What's he done now?"

"Nothing really. Got falling-down drunk, and the bartender called to have us come scoop him up off the floor. Hit his head somewhere along the way. We just thought we'd have it checked out before we called someone to come get him. How'd you know where to find him?"

"I wasn't really looking for him. I was upstairs visiting a friend. I saw you bringing him in."

Felix swore colorfully, then added, "Arrest me!"

"Hush, Felix."

"Don't hush me. I hate being hushed. *You* hush once in a while. See how you like it."

"Oh, for crying out loud."

"Arrest me! Arrest me! Arrest me!" he said, when Bobby was called from the room by his partner.

"Felix!"

"That junkyard dog is going to eat me alive if you don't. You want that? You'd probably like that, wouldn't you?" he asked Ellen. "Just let him get me. Sweep old Felix under the carpet and get him out of your way. Well, if you don't make them arrest me, that's exactly what's going to happen. Your wish will come true. The junkyard dog is gonna get me. He'll hunt me down and get me."

"What junkyard dog?"

"*The* junkyard dog. The only junkyard dog in the only junkyard in town."

She frowned, confused. Tom Krane owned the only junkyard in town. And he had a dog that would hunt Felix down and . . . ? No. Tom Krane *was* the junkyard dog. And Felix's moneylender? That's who Felix was so afraid of? Tom Krane?

"Felix. Calm down. Nobody is going to hurt you."

By the time the last word was out of her mouth, Felix was screaming deliriously at the top of his lungs, pulling at his restraints, and thrashing his legs. Over and over she tried to get through to him, but fear fueled by alcohol made him unreachable.

"Okay, fine," she said, about the time Bobby and his partner and a nurse came into the room. "Arrest him. Take him off to jail. Throw away the key." Only part of her was being facetious.

"Ellen, he hasn't done anything."

"Are you kidding? Listen to him. He's disturbing the peace. He's a public nuisance. He's drunk and disorderly. He's intoxicated in public. He's dirty. He's a pain in my . . ." She stopped when she realized she might be going too far. She let loose a big sigh. "Look, Bobby, maybe arresting him would be good for him. He shouldn't be allowed to wake up in my mother's guest room every time he does this. He should wake up uncomfortable and spend time in jail, with nothing to drink but water. It might do him good."

"He'd only be there overnight."

"Then what happens? You just turn him loose?"

"Pretty much. We write him a ticket with a fine attached to it. He can contest it in court if he wants to, but most of them don't."

"What happens if he can't pay the fine?" she asked, thinking a few days in a sobering situation like that might be just what Felix needed to make a rehabilitation center a little more appealing to him.

"We let him go anyway, on his own recognizance. He has sixty days to pay the fine."

"What if he still doesn't pay the fine?" She was just curious.

"Then, if we want to make an issue of it, we can haul him up in front of a judge, who can either throw him back in jail or sentence him to rehabilitation, if he thinks it would do any good. People his age," he motioned with his head toward Felix, "they usually get sentenced to rehab if they express a desire to go and a willingness to give it try. But . . . well, when they go that route, it's on their record. Permanently. He's awfully young—"

"He's awfully sick, Bobby." She looked back at her brother, who was now quietly flirting with the nurse. "And I don't know how else to help him."

Bobby had been right earlier, about high school being a long time gone for them. She watched him consider the pros and cons of arresting her brother and didn't notice even the slightest remains of the boy he'd once been. Still tall, but lean now instead of skinny, he had a serious, self-assured countenance that didn't seem at all affected by what he'd once felt for her. His attention was focused on Felix and his job and the best solution for both.

"At least he wasn't driving," he said, finally. "If we tap him for drunk-and-disorderly, it won't be so bad."

"Thank you, Bobby," she said, thinking it a stupid thing to say when he was about to arrest her brother. But all in all, it seemed like the best course for everyone involved—*except* Bobby, who now had to make an arrest and do all the paperwork. Felix, in his present pickled state, would feel safer. Her mother and her sister wouldn't need to hear or worry about it until morning. And she would have time to work something out with Mr. Krane.

"Bobby, you're a good man," Felix was saying, delighted to be going to jail. "Thanks for arresting me on such short notice like this. You can untie me now. I'll go peaceably. I won't even try to escape. You won't regret this. I'll be a model inmate."

"Shut up, Felix," she and Bobby said in unison. Bobby moved to untie the restraints.

"I hope you're happy now. You've embarrassed both of us here tonight," she hissed at him.

"Well, don't you worry about me," he said bravely. "I can handle it. And Krane will never think to look for me in jail."

"Krane?" Bobby asked, frowning and showing concern as he worked on the knot. "Are you in trouble with Tom Krane?"

"No, no," Felix was quick to reassure him, narrowing his eyes at his sister as a warning to be silent. "No trouble. Just a little misunderstanding. Nothing serious."

"Stay away from him, Felix," Bobby said, removing the last restraint. "He's bad news. Steer clear of him."

Felix rolled his eyes and wagged his head. "What do you think I've been trying to do here all night?"

"Ellen?"

"What? Oh. I'm sorry," she said a while later, sitting next to Jonah in a small booth at a fast-food restaurant. "What were you saying?"

He smiled his forgiveness. "I was saying that you've been awfully quiet and distracted since we left the hospital. Is something wrong?"

"No," she said automatically. "What could be wrong? I . . ." Her gaze met his, and she was instantly lost in time and space. In the back of her mind she knew he had the strength to break her in half if he wanted to—but there was such a gentleness about him. She wasn't sure if it was because she knew his history or simply sensed it, but sometimes she had the feeling he had an inexhaustible reserve of this same gentleness, and so much more, all wrapped up with a shiny ribbon, ready to give—but not to just anyone. To her alone. It was as if he'd traveled through time, eon after eon, waiting and searching for her, specifically. It was a huge responsibility and a comfort at once. Exciting and soothing in turn. Empowering, yet it was his blind acceptance of her worthiness that she valued the most. "I'm here with you. And to tell you the truth, nothing else seems to matter much. We barely know each other, but I feel as if . . ."

"As if we've known each other forever?"

"No, not at all," she said, with a small laugh and a look of surprise. A feeling like that would have been so simple and easy to explain. She slipped her hand between his and the tabletop in front of them. His fingers

curled around it instantly, warm and secure. "You're
not like anyone or anything I've known before. You're
not even . . . what I dreamed of. You're . . ."

There were no words. She looked into his eyes and
prayed he could see in hers what she was trying to say.
She'd never known someone like him even existed,
much less imagined the possibility. Maybe she'd simply
never allowed herself the hope of finding someone who
would speak in places deep in her heart, places that she
had always assumed would remain hollow and empty,
echoing throughout time, unnoticed and unap-
preciated.

A raging forest fire couldn't come close to generat-
ing the heat in his expression, or cause such devastation
in her heart. He moved closer, kissed her tenderly,
seeming to understand—to accept that there was no
real explanation for why or how one loved another, it
simply was.

"Thank you," he said, his face still close enough for
kissing.

"For what?"

"For tonight. For last night. For being you." He
punctuated each phrase with a kiss. "I don't know if I
believe in fate, but it wasn't just my father who brought
me to this town."

She smiled, recognizing the thought. "I know."

Because she knew, because she made it all so easy
for him, and because he needed to, he kissed her, deeply
and greedily. This time there was no holding back, no
deferring to the newness of the relationship or the
qualms of revealing all he truly was—possessive, force-
ful, demanding. A tiny helpless moan of surrender
aroused his killer instincts. He was poised to move in
for the kill when he heard it again and reined himself

in. With the small smacking noise of their lips parting ringing in his ears, he held her away from him. She was so beautiful, and so *his* . . . his heart contracted painfully in his chest, his lungs seized. There was nothing more he wanted from the world than to take her, devour her—except to cherish and indulge her.

This might have been the time, but it wasn't the place.

"I better get you home," he said, swallowing hard.

"Back to your place?" Such a wild feral light came to his eyes that her breath caught in her throat. In one of those unreal moments that didn't have anything to do with anything, she recalled hearing that the tiny little hearts of chipmunks and squirrels were known to beat so hard and so fast in times of great excitement or fear that they sometimes exploded, and wondered vaguely if that same phenomenon could or had ever happened to a human. Unconsciously she reached to calm hers. "My car. It's at your house. I followed you home."

He closed his eyes, then chuckled silently at himself. "Yes," he said, smiling back. "Yes. Yes, it is. Yes, you did. Yes."

They both knew and rejoiced in the fact that a deed half done wasn't done at all. Their time would come.

CHAPTER SIX

STEP SIX

Whether you think you can
or think you can't, you're right.
—Henry Ford

The power of positive thinking far exceeds that of a
hydrogen bomb. It cures diseases, discovers new worlds,
takes pictures of Mars, and, in general, makes you feel
just fine. Try it. Be that Little Engine that could.
Think you can, and you will.

She woke up humming. She had her whole day planned before she had her eyes open.

Ellen figured there were good points and not so good points to every season that passed through Quincey—hence she had no favorite. Winter was cold but beautiful, peaceful. Spring was fresh and new; unpredictable and soggy at the same time. Fall was busy and dying at once. And summer was hot and hotter with a scattering of days that were so perfect, they renewed the soul and made life a pure joy.

It was one of those days—the pure joy kind. The sky was a bright, bright blue with fluffy white cotton clouds drifting slow and lazy from west to east. Pushing them was a cool soft breeze that kept the *t-e-r* from connecting with *hot*, as it rustled the leaves in the trees. Birds sang and flowers perfumed the air. Felix was safe and sober, albeit hungover, in jail. Her mother was planning to bail him out at noon and take him home while Ellen straightened things out with Tom Krane. But best of all, she was in love—and she and Jonah had rescheduled their dinner for that night.

All in all, a perfect summer day. Felix was safe, her heart was full of love, and the little green book predicted success—she was thinking that a little artful seduction was in order. Either that or she was going to start gnawing on the furniture. She'd tossed and turned the whole night through, waking fully once or twice to wonder if her restlessness was due to Felix's imbroglio or the titillating dreams she incurred whether her eyes were closed or not.

She hadn't actually done much seducing in the past. Too-nice people tended not to be vamps. But she'd been to the movies and had a general idea of the concept, and with the looks Jonah had given her the previous night, and the kisses . . . well, how hard could it be? Besides, Jonah was taking too long. If she'd kissed any other man the way she'd kissed him, at the very least some serious groping would have occurred by now. But not with Jonah. Oh, he wanted her, a doorknob could see he wanted her. But despite the intimacy of his kisses and the controlled passion in his eyes, his hands and his manner had been nothing but gentle and tender and respectful.

She buttoned the button and zipped the zipper on her dark moss-green slacks and didn't miss the cunning grin on her face when she stepped in front the mirror to check the fit. She hadn't missed the I've-had-sex-around-the-world-in-eighty-days-and-you've-never-been-outside-Indiana disposition he'd displayed either. An excited giggle escaped her. Experience wasn't everything. He'd have a whole new perspective and a different kind of respect for her after tonight.

She was going to love him so hard and so well, he'd blank out every other encounter he'd ever had. She was going to love him so deeply and so generously that he'd forget every moment he'd ever spent alone and lonely. She was going to love him so totally, he'd be able to feel her in every cell of his body and he'd never again know where he ended and she began . . . or vice versa.

With the matching dark moss-green jacket hung over one arm, she was dumping the contents of one purse into another when she thought she heard a soft rapping at her door.

"Mrs. Phipps," she said when she opened the door, a strange mix of surprise and alarm washing over her. She rarely came to her door, because Ellen spent a great deal of time in Mrs. Phipps's apartment, but also because climbing stairs was hard for her. "What are you doing up here? I thought we agreed you wouldn't use the stairs unless someone was with you?"

"Oh, I'm fine," the old woman said, smiling a bit. She didn't look fine, she looked ill at ease. "We just wanted to thank you for leaving our things by our door when you came in last night. We were still up, we heard you. We guessed you just didn't want to disturb us at that hour."

To save time, Ellen fastened up her purse and slipped on her jacket while she asked, "Are you having trouble sleeping?"

"None at all. We were just awake." She watched as Ellen held Bubba out of her apartment with one foot while reaching for the door to close it. "We brought you a warm muffin," Mrs. Phipps said, an uncommon timidity in her voice. She held up a dishcloth-covered plate that Ellen hadn't noticed till then. "Blueberry. Our favorite."

"Oh. Thank you," she said, taking the plate. And again to save time, she took the old lady's arm and turned her toward the staircase. "Here, let me help you back down. I'm running a little late this morning, but I'll take this with me. I'll thank you again during my coffee break."

"We thought you had a little more time yet. You don't usually leave this early," the woman said, stepping down slowly and carefully, so unsure of each step that they might as well have been moving. "We thought some tea and a muffin . . ."

"Oh, no," Ellen said with a small laugh, gently supporting her and trying hard not to hurry the old bones down to the landing. She knew *no* was enough, that an explanation wasn't necessary, but this was Mrs. Phipps, after all. "I don't really have time for tea this morning. I'm going in early because I want some extra time at lunch for some errands I want to run. . . ." And, recalling that Mrs. Phipps was the Queen of Errands, she added, "I don't have a minute to spare today."

"Oh."

Every rule in the little green book flashed through

her mind, and still she couldn't stop herself. "Can I have a rain check on that tea?"

"Yes. Yes, of course, dear. We're always happy to see you. Any time you have free, we'll have tea."

"Thanks, Mrs. Phipps. And thanks for the muffin," she said, lifting the dish towel once they'd reached level ground. With muffin in hand, she hurried down the hall toward the back of the house, calling, "Have a good day, Mrs. Phipps."

"Quincey First Federal. This is Ellen," she announced into the telephone. It was midmorning and already the people of Quincey were showing frequent signs of stress and concern over their finances. Ellen was worried about them. "How may I help you today?"

"You can come across the street and let me kiss you, for a start."

There was half a second of panic and confusion before the voice registered. She laughed.

"I'd love to, but I haven't even had time for a coffee break this morning," she said, eyeing the crumby remnants of Mrs. Phipps's muffin on the tissue in front of her.

"I noticed. I almost brought you a cup, to help wash down your muffin."

"My . . ." She laughed and swiveled her chair to the big picture window. Across the street he waved his cordless phone at her. "Is your eyesight that good? Or have you been using binoculars?"

"If I had, I'd know what *kind* of muffin it was."

"Blueberry."

"Ah. Thank you, that was driving me nuts."

They grinned at each other. There were a lot of

things driving them nuts; the distance between the bank and the camera shop was definitely one of them.

"Guess what I found out this morning," he said. He almost shuddered at how eager he sounded. Sharing wasn't exactly his forte, but he could hardly contain himself. So strange, it was as if his left hand were telling his right hand what it was doing, what it was feeling and sensing, as if he needed to share with her to feel balanced and more coordinated, to feel whole.

"What?"

"I stopped by to check on my father this morning, to see if the doctor had anything new to say."

"And?"

"And he didn't, but that's not it. What I called you about."

"Okay." She waited expectantly.

"His nurse came in while I was there and started cleaning up his room, you know, putting his bath things away and getting ready to change the sheets and throwing out dead flowers. . . ." He hesitated, as excited about his news as he was about sharing it. "So I thanked her, for the flowers."

"Why?"

An incredulous noise. "I thought she'd been bringing them. Her or some charity organization, or a group of little old ladies who bring flowers to sick people to cheer them up. Sick people with no families—"

"You didn't bring them?"

"No, I . . . I didn't think . . ." He didn't think his father would notice or appreciate flowers. "No. I wish I had."

"So, who's been bringing them? I don't think nurses do that."

"They don't usually," he said with a small laugh.

"She thought I was crazy. Told me that if nurses brought flowers to every sick person they cared for, there wouldn't be a single bloom left on the face of the planet."

"Who's been bringing them, then?"

"Well," he said, rather pleased with his investigative results, "apparently my father has a lady visitor every afternoon."

"Really?"

"Yep. I sometimes check on him in the morning and I usually go every evening, but since I opened the shop, I've been skipping afternoon visiting hours. It never occurred to me that anyone else had been visiting him."

She smiled at him through the window. "So you'll be taking a long lunch today too."

"Too?"

"I have some errands to run."

"Oh. Yes. Late too. Afternoon visiting hours are from two to four."

"Aren't you dying to know who it is? I am," she said, the excitement in her bubbling in her voice. "I won't be able to think of anything else till I know."

He laughed. "You have three lines blinking there. Get back to work. I'll call you later, as soon as I know."

"Okay. Jonah?"

"Yes?"

"I'm looking forward to tonight."

His smile flashed in the window across the street. She squinted. It was a deep-down happy smile. She'd seen it before. He used it every time he was deep-down happy, whether it had anything to do with her or not.

"Me too. See you later."

"You're making it way too easy for him," Vi said, stepping around the petition before Ellen could connect to a blinking light. "Men like a little chase before they catch their prey."

Ellen cast her friend a torpid glance, pushed a red button, and made her announcement, then added, "Do you have that account number handy, Mrs. Walker? Good. One moment please." She put Mrs. Walker on hold and while she looked up her account on the computer, said, "It's not like that, Vi. We don't need to play games. We don't want to. We like being honest with each other. Telling each other what's on our mind, how we feel . . . it's . . . I don't know. It feels so natural and right to be with him. Mrs. Walker? Yes, check number seven-fifty-two was written for the amount of $45.67 on July seventh. Yes, ma'am. You're welcome." She pushed another button and repeated the procedure. "I've never felt this way before. It's different than anything I've ever known."

Vi smiled, though her expression was thoughtful as she studied her friend's face. "Good for you, kiddo. I'm glad for you. In fact . . . you look"—a vague shake of her head—"different. New vitamins? Or is it love?"

Ellen giggled. "Yes. I think so." And she thought of her little green book. "And more. A new outlook on life."

Vi's brows rose with interest. "What triggered this spontaneous evolution?"

She glanced out the window. "He did. And you did. You helped. You were right, you know. I used to be way too nice. I'm standing up for myself now. Taking what I want. It feels great."

"Like the loan officer position when Mary has her baby?"

"Yes. I told Joleen I'd quit if I didn't get it."

"Did you know Lisa Lee was interested in it too?"

"Sure. But I have seniority. I should have it."

"I didn't know you were all that interested in loans," she said, a furrow forming between her eyes.

"I'm not. But it's not like it's a permanent position. And it can't hurt to know that stuff. Don't worry. I won't leave you here to handle customer service alone for very long."

"That's not what I'm worried about," she said. There was an odd tone in her voice as she slipped back around the petition.

Ellen thought she almost sounded angry, but about what? The blinking lights were multiplying like rabbits on her phone. She shrugged and pushed another button.

Vi wasn't going to be any happier with her when she didn't come back from lunch on time on such a busy day, but that couldn't be helped. Neither of her errands were the emergencies she'd told Joleen about, but with the right attitude those little white lies that never really hurt anyone and that everyone resorted to now and again were becoming easier and easier to tell people. Besides, how many times had she covered for Vi over the years? A hundred zillion times? She'd get over it.

Especially if Ellen showed her what her first mission had accomplished.

Most days Gerald's Ladies' Apparel was a little too rich for Ellen's tastes, and particularly for her pocket-book. But today it was the only place to go to get what she wanted. And Vi would wholeheartedly approve when she told her she'd finally bought something there. Vi swore they had a better selection of ladies' lingerie than most of the X-rated catalogues she subscribed to.

Sure enough, in less than thirty minutes she was in the fitting room, a teal blue negligee slinking over her skin like something spun by elves and sprinkled with fairy dust. She stood sideways in the mirror, one shoulder of the robe drifting loose to her elbow, her hair full and curly, her eyes bright . . . and she smiled. She didn't look too nice now. She looked like a well-equipped femme fatale. A temptress.

Her heart fluttered with nerves and excitement. Jonah may have been around the block a few more times than she had, but his wandering days were over. She giggled at her reflection. Who would have believed that someone as nice as she was could ever harbor such wantonness? Not that she was actually wanton; she wouldn't know where to begin to be genuinely wanton. She was just crazy in love and acting like it, doing what came naturally. Maybe that was the difference, then. Maybe she'd never loved anyone else enough to wrap herself in shimmering teal blue silk and give herself to them like a gift—heart, soul, and body. Maybe she'd never thought of herself as being special enough or unique enough to be a gift before. . . .

With the black and silver shopping bag from Gerald's in hand, she walked out onto the sidewalk, sucked in a lungful of that oh-so-perfect day, then chugged right along to her next assignment. *I think I can. I think I can. I know I can* pumped through her brain as she drove by the bank and the camera shop again, beyond the street she lived on, farther than the turnoff to the hospital, and then a few more miles until she pulled into the parking lot of a place called Krane's Krap. Junk, Junk, and More Junk, the sign said.

The Town Council had been after Tom Krane to change the name of his establishment for as long as she

could remember. It was the misspelling of the second
word that invariably put a halt to the legal actions taken
against him. As children, she and Jane and Felix would
herald their every sighting of the place by reading the
signs, out loud and in unison, to make their mother
cringe—and because it was just plain fun to say.

She still smiled every time she drove by. You had to
respect a man who would dare such a thing in the first
place, then defend it for so long. And she knew Tom
Krane a bit from his dealings with the bank. Though
not exactly someone she'd choose as a bosom buddy, he
was a practical man who refinanced his loans when interest rates dropped enough to make a significant difference in his payments, and he made no effort to hide
the fact that he didn't appreciate the bank's service
charges. In fact, Joleen had taken to quoting him in her
sporadic pep talks. "All our customers are thinking,
'When I pay a service fee, I expect some service.' "

Personally, the few times she'd waited on him, he'd
seemed like a gruff but reasonable man. It was his rea-
soning she would address today, she reminded herself,
as she opened the door to the front office.

It wasn't the sort of place women frequented.
Therefore no concessions were made to aesthetics or
cleanliness or order or anything else the female of the
species generally contributed to the civilized world.
Without mincing words, it was poorly lit, filthy, smelly,
and, in general, a dump.

Stepping gingerly, as if she might step in a pile of
testosterone and ruin her shoes, she approached a
burly, unshaven gentleman sitting on a rusty stool behind a makeshift counter made of plywood.

"Ma'am."

"Hi." She cleared her throat of the I-don't-belong-

here-but sound and replaced it with a don't-give-me-
attitude-cuz-I-know-how-it-works tone of voice. "I'd
like to speak with Mr. Krane if he isn't busy."

Busy doing what? she wondered. Sweeping the
junkyard out back? Rearranging piles of rusty metal?
Sorting hubcaps maybe?

"Yes, ma'am," he said. And then in a booming voice
that shook the boards under her feet, he bellowed,
"Tom!"

"Yeah," a voice boomed back, and the boards vi-
brated in another direction.

"Woman here to see you," he said, with the same
amount of air that it would have taken him to say
"Someone here to see you." But no. And he said *woman*
with the same intonation he might have used for the
word *alien* or *invader* or . . . *Purple People Eater*.

Now, she wouldn't have sworn to it, mind you—she
wasn't good at waiting under the best of circum-
stances—but it seemed to her that no matter what he
was doing, he could have come, handled their business,
and been gone again, ten times over, in the time it took
Tom Krane to make an appearance. It also seemed as if
his slowness were deliberate, but she wouldn't have
sworn to it.

However, he was pleasant enough when he finally
arrived.

"I know you from somewhere," he said, frowning at
her from the doorway behind the burly man on the
stool.

"The bank, Mr. Krane. Quincey First Federal," she
said, in case he patronized more than one bank. She
wanted to make this as simple, clear, and to-the-point
as possible. She sensed he'd appreciate it. "I'm Ellen
Webster. I've waited on you several times."

"Webster," he said, obviously recognizing the name.

"That's right. I'm here to see you about the money my brother owes you."

He was a tall, thin man who despite the summer heat was wearing a plaid flannel shirt over a gray T-shirt with jeans. Physically he didn't look as if he could crush a beer can, but there was something in the way he stood and angled his head that told her if she believed that, she was sorely mistaken. His eyes were hooded and narrow and keen . . . and intimidating when aimed directly at her.

"I don't know your brother."

She glanced at the burly man who sat on the stool with his arms crossed over his large belly, not moving away to give them privacy or looking to Krane for instructions. He seemed to think he belonged in the conversation. They both did. So she went on.

"He knows you. And he knows he owes you money. He also knows you'll hurt him if he doesn't pay it back."

"That's extortion, ma'am. That's against the law." He wasn't denying anything, he was just stating the facts. "Course, to me, it's no different than the bank foreclosing on a car or a house or . . ." he looked around, ". . . a business if the loan payments aren't made. But I don't make the laws. I just live by 'em."

It occurred to her suddenly that the cagey, distrustful air about him might be due to a suspicion that she was wearing a wire or working with the police against him, and she almost laughed. What would he do to Felix if he thought he'd turned him in? Or her for that matter?

"I know you do," she said as sincerely as she could,

relying on her newfound guilt-free attitude toward lying to get her through and make her sound convincing. "And I appreciate you not going to the authorities about this. Felix owes you a lot of money. He could go to jail for a long time. He . . . we both appreciate the time you've given him to pay off his debt to you. But the thing is, he has no money. He has no job. Nothing to sell. No savings. And even if we—his family—were willing to help him, we couldn't come up with that kind of money."

Choosing his words carefully, he asked, "If your brother did owe money to someone, you wouldn't help him? No one in your family would?"

Did he know what an easy touch her mother was?

"No one in the family *could*. Even if they knew about it, they couldn't," she said, hoping to inspire trust with her secrecy.

"Sounds like your brother's got himself into a real pickle, then, don't it? Whoever he owes that money to isn't going to be happy if he doesn't pay them back, you know."

"I do know. And I wouldn't blame them for being unhappy." She hesitated. "Anything else I'd blame them for, of course," she said as she shook her head, a silent plea for her brother's safety. "That's why I thought maybe you could give me some advice or make a suggestion as to the best way to work something like this out with someone." He stared at her in silence. "Now I was thinking of some sort of . . . oh, work-related situation. Something where my brother could work off what he owes, say, right here at the junkyard. He gets paid a minimum wage, pays off his debt, so much a week. That sort of thing."

He scratched his head through his close-clipped

hair. "And why should I be willing to help your brother pay off his debt?"

Good question.

"Well, because you're a good businessman. I've always thought this about you. And . . ."—how was she going to word this?—". . . if my brother's healthy enough to work and pay off his debt at the same time, then you . . . um . . . you . . ."

"I'd have his undying gratitude?"

"That's right. And everyone would be getting something. You'd be getting a loyal employee. Whoever Felix owes the money to would get paid off. And Felix would be safe and get out of debt." Somehow that seemed to work out just fine.

He studied her for a minute that seemed to go on forever. When he finally spoke, his words were calculated.

"Well now, to be honest with you, I don't really need any new help around here. I got my brother-in-law here." The burly man on the stool. "He's a ball of energy. And your brother's debts aren't my problem. But I like you. It's plain you care for your brother and you got spunk coming here to get him a job. So, I'll tell you what," he said, pushing away from the doorjamb, preparing to leave. "You send that brother of yours around here tomorrow evening, about closing time. I'll show him around the place. He can start working the morning after."

I thought I could. I thought I could. I knew I could.

"Oh, thank you, Mr. Krane. You won't regret this. This was a good, sound business decision. I'll make sure Felix is here tomorrow," she said, moving toward the door to leave. Wanting to dance a little jig they would never understand. "Six o'clock sharp. Thank you.

Thank you very much." She glanced away, reaching for the doorknob, and when she looked back, he was gone. Only the unshaven man on the rusty metal stool remained. "Thank you too."

Across the dusty unpaved street from Krane's Krap—Junk, Junk, and More Junk—Jonah sat in his leased sedan with a frown on his face, waiting for her to emerge from the junkyard's office.

She'd zoomed past him forty-five minutes earlier as he'd been pulling out of the lot behind the bank on his way to the hospital, about one o'clock. He been so excited to meet the woman who'd been visiting his father, he didn't want to be late and miss her. So he'd closed the shop an hour earlier than necessary, ignoring the little voice inside him that was telling him he was being foolish and overreacting. He'd honked at Ellen but she hadn't heard him, her mind clearly on something else— her driving, her destination? He wished he knew.

He wished he knew everything about her. Not that he wasn't enjoying getting to know her a little at time, but . . . well, there it was. It was his instinct to discover all there was to know about most anything, and Ellen was a very important something. He'd studied, probed, investigated, collected data on hundreds and hundreds of people, places, and things, none of them nearly as important to him or as interesting to him as Ellen.

He'd turned onto the street in front of the bank and could still see her several blocks ahead. He'd grinned and given in easily to the impulse to follow her. When she got to wherever she was going, it was his plan to jump out of his car, say hi, and steal the kiss he'd been craving all morning. A little spontaneous romance he thought he'd try his hand at. She was worth it.

When they'd driven past the turnoff to the hospital, he'd glanced at his watch. Still plenty of time to get that kiss, he'd thought. But when she'd slowed down and pulled into Krane's Krap, he'd pulled to the side of the dirt road and merely sat there, too baffled to move.

He'd watched her straighten out her clothes, smooth her hair, then throw her shoulders back as if she needed a little extra courage. She'd approached the shabby building slowly, entered with caution—it wasn't a place she frequented and she wasn't comfortable frequenting it now.

He didn't like the feeling closing in on his chest like a vice or the grip in the pit of stomach. They were familiar enough to him and they didn't bode well. He recognized them as early warning signals for trouble and danger—and in this situation pure terror, with Ellen involved.

He leaned back in his seat, his hands gripping the steering wheel. If it weren't for the twisting and churning inside him, he'd have driven away, not wanting her to think he was spying on her but . . . There was no way he could do that now. He had two choices left. Go insane waiting for her to come out. Or join her inside.

He looked at his watch again. It was one forty-five. She was about fifty minutes late for work. Stopping at the junkyard was important to her, then, because she was rarely more than five or ten minutes late getting back from lunch. His father's mystery woman would have to wait. He scanned the vicinity with a practiced eye. The street was quiet; there was no one in sight. He'd give Ellen fifteen minutes to come out of there, or he was going in.

In the next fourteen minutes he tapped the crystal of his watch three different times to make sure it was working. His hand was poised on the door handle and he was about to renege on the last minute of her grace period when he heard the door squeak open across the street. She came out empty-handed but smiling—even though she hurried over to her car in a fashion that suggested more than just being late for work.

He started the car and drove up the road a fair distance, then watched in his rearview mirror as her car emerged from the junkyard and turned down the street in the opposite direction. He pulled a U-turn and went back.

She was safe and unharmed, but he still couldn't shake the monkey off his back. Something was wrong. Something she hadn't told him about. He could feel it in his bones. Why hadn't she told him? Because it was something minor? Because she could handle it alone? Was it sticky and embarrassing? She didn't know how to tell him? She didn't trust him? Maybe she didn't even know she was in trouble?

An act of God couldn't have stopped him from pulling into the junkyard lot. He wouldn't be able to breathe right until he'd assessed the situation himself. Okay, so maybe he was butting in where he might not belong. He'd take his lumps for it later. No problem. He'd still be able to look at himself in the mirror.

The man on the rusty metal stool didn't bat an eye during his inane story of being a visitor in town with a license plate collection. The tall skinny guy waved him through, past the makeshift counter and through a huge storage area to a bin and small display of license plates from various states. They talked man-to-man about the heat and where he was from and why he was in town, the man's interest in Ford pickup trucks and the hazards of tire piles, while he sifted through the plates.

Three quarters of an hour later he was driving away with a 1958 licence plate from Kansas and a puzzle he couldn't solve.

He couldn't imagine why Ellen had gone there in the first place. Or why she'd been so obviously uncomfortable about it. The men inside weren't overtly suspicious, but seemed to exude trouble the same way they might garlic on their breath. But there was nothing concrete, nothing he could put a finger on. It was all gut feelings and subtle observations.

CHAPTER SEVEN

STEP SEVEN

Fill what's empty. Empty what's full.
Scratch where it itches.
—*Alice Roosevelt Longworth*

Just do it.

"Well, who is she? What did she say?" she wanted to know when Jonah called as he'd promised to, later in the afternoon. "I've been sitting here on pins and needles all afternoon."

Actually it felt more like she had ants in her pants than needles in her chair, she was so excited. And not just about Earl Blake's mystery woman. About everything. It was all coming together perfectly.

She had Felix's problem solved. She had Jonah and a negligee in his favorite *gray* in the black and silver shopping bag at her feet. She had a pay raise coming and a possible short-term promotion in the works. She was a woman in control of her life. She was taking what she wanted from the world. What more could she ask for . . . except maybe a marriage proposal and a move to Washington, D.C.? She laughed silently and squirmed in her chair. That was a secret wish that had suddenly popped out of its box, but there it was. It was too late to stuff it back in the box and put it back on the shelf. Impulsively she flipped the latch on the box of another secret wish and included children and then grandchildren to her list.

All right, so she'd been a little ambivalent about the little green book at first. Who in their right mind wouldn't have been? But now? Now she was a believer. The advice inside it had worked too often for it to be mere coincidence. With that little book in hand, there was nothing she couldn't do. She looked out the big bank window. Her future was like the sun, bright and vital—her eyes made contact with Jonah's—and wonderful.

"Tell me everything," she said, speaking once again of the mystery woman Jonah had just met.

"I will, I promise, but later. There's just too much to tell you now. Your phone looks like it's on fire over there." She didn't look or sound as if anything untoward had happened to her that afternoon. Maybe his suspicions were unfounded? Maybe he was imagining things earlier?

She glanced at the lights, flashing and blinking. "Okay. But at least tell me who she is. I have to know."

He chuckled. "Denise Gunther is her name. Mr. Gunther's daughter-in-law. The soldier's wife."

"You're kidding." She laughed. "Oh, you know what? I'll bet she was in the phone book all along."

He groaned. "I know. I thought the same thing afterward and felt really stupid. I didn't even think about looking up *his* relatives." There was a short pause. "Maybe I didn't think I'd care about what they might know about him. My father, I mean."

He had his head lowered in the window across the street; she couldn't see his face.

"You care now, Jonah. That's what counts."

His head came up slowly. He looked back at her for several long seconds, then admitted, "I do care now. About a lot of things."

She smiled and he smiled back. She squinted. It was half an I-knew-you'd-understand and half a thank-you smile. It coated her heart with warm satisfaction.

"I know you do," she said. "I think you always have."

There was a thoughtful silence before he spoke again.

"You think so, huh?" he said in a light teasing tone, as he blinked away an absurd urge to shed water from his eyes. "What do you think I'm feeling right now?"

She knew this smile instantly, and she laughed. "That's easy. The same thing I'm feeling right now."

His chuckle sent chills up her spine. "In that case, hang on to that feeling. We'll be picking this conversation up again later. Oh. That reminds me. Would you mind eating out tonight, instead of at the house? I found an interesting looking seafood place this afternoon, and I feel like celebrating."

"I do too."

Ellen rode her perfect-day buzz well into the afternoon. But by the time she left work and the sun was hanging low in the sky, the intense elation had metamorphosed to a deep contentment, one of those too rare times of profound gratitude simply to be alive. She moved slowly, sucking in the scents of summer, tuned in to the aerial songs of the larks, and the grass growing under her feet.

"Can we help you with anything, dear?" came Mrs. Phipps's weak but still shrill voice from the screened porch that served as the back entrance to their apartment house. "We've been watching for you."

She sighed happily. "No, Mrs. Phipps, I don't need any help today," she said, climbing the wooden stairs and stepping over Bubba, seated smack in the middle of the doorway. Her benevolence swelled to include the old woman and the cat. It was nice to be watched for, nice being cared about, good to have friends. "How are you feeling today?"

"We're fine, dear. We were just thinking of having some tea, a fine way to end a busy day and begin a quiet evening, we think."

She smiled. A few solid, predictable events in your life were nice too. She reached out and patted her shoulder fondly, then turned to go up the stairs to her apartment.

"Enjoy your tea, Mrs. Phipps."

"But, Ellen . . . we . . . we were hoping you would join us. Tea is for two."

"No," she said kindly. *No explanations needed. No excuses required.* "Not tonight."

She thought about adding "Thanks anyway" or "Maybe some other time," but the longer she stood there talking, the more opportunities Mrs. Phipps would have to bring up her shopping list or an errand she wanted run—and those days were over. Well, for the most part anyway. She wasn't thinking of *never* helping, or *never* shopping for her, or *never* having tea with her again. She wasn't cruel, she just wasn't so very, very nice anymore.

"Oh," she heard the old woman say, and she continued up the stairs. "That's fine. Another time perhaps."

Ellen smiled. Good ol' Mrs. Phipps. She should have known she'd understand.

Nearing the top step, she heard the distinctive squeak of a door and her gaze darted to Eugene's. It was cracked slightly; she could see the iridescent green light from his computer shining through the slit.

"Forget it, Eugene," she said, saving herself some time and him the effort of leaving his apartment. "My cupboards are bare and I'm eating out tonight. Seafood," she added, to warn him against waiting for a doggy bag. "Salmonella, you know."

The door squeaked closed again.

Was life grand or what?

Unlocking the door to her apartment, she spotted fat Bubba at her feet, waiting patiently to go in. It niggled at the back of her mind that he wasn't her cat and she didn't have to have cat hair on her couch if she didn't want it there. But . . . well, he was a cat after all. He wouldn't understand being locked out. Mildly resenting that which was still a little too nice in her, she opened the door wide to him.

"Your days in here are numbered, pal," she told him. "So watch where you drop your hair, okay?"

Like a butterfly flitting from flower to flower in the sunshine, she picked up here, straightened there, fluffed this, patted that, until her little apartment was just the way she wanted it, neat and cozy. Then like a spider, she moved from bedroom to bath, spinning her seductive web.

Her skin tingled and her heart fluttered thinking of

it. She folded the thin teal blue silk carefully in tissue paper. She emptied most everything out of her handbag and carefully placed the negligee inside it, using her wallet and sunglasses case to keep it from sliding and crumpling at the bottom. She threw in perfume and an extra toothbrush. She wasn't sure where it would happen, only that it would, and she wanted to be prepared.

Of course, there was every chance in the world she wouldn't need half of it. Her breath came quick and a bit ragged, thinking of a first encounter that was all hot wet kissing and the shredding of clothes. But it caught in her throat and her heart thumped hard and painfully as she dreamt of a slow, sensuous, shared seduction. She sighed, slipping chin deep into a tepid bubble bath that cooled her skin, soothed her muscles, and touched something very feminine in her soul.

Who would have thought Ellen Webster could feel so good? Not that she'd actually been suffering a horrible, tortured life before. She hadn't. Her life had been okay—but just okay. She simply hadn't known life could feel so good. Didn't know a little control could awaken the power and the courage to take more control. Wasn't aware that love could heighten all the senses, make life seem so much more precious and valuable.

As for the niggling little nit of guilt that wheedled its way to her consciousness now and then, she easily squelched it. It was her right to be happy. She deserved to be happy. She didn't have to let people walk all over her. She didn't have to sit quietly by while others took what belonged to her. Didn't have to help them prosper. She didn't have to shop for and have tea with someone just because they were old and sweet. Didn't have to feed the lazy and strange. She didn't have to do anything she didn't want to do. Didn't have to do anything that wasn't in her own best interests. This was her life, and in it, she was the only one who mattered.

And so it was that when she opened the door to Jonah a short time later, she wasn't feeling self-conscious but extremely conscious of self. She had an itch she wanted scratched and a man she loved and wanted to possess. She deserved to have everything she wanted. It was her right to be happy.

Every atom of her body was singing its own rendition of Helen Reddy's "I Am Woman." The long cotton gauze dress she wore swirled and brushed against her skin like a hundred little feathers. The breeze through the open window kissed the back of her neck like a lover. Her heart was fluttering like the wings of a hummingbird—not with fear or anxiety but with excitement and determination. She was all tingles and goose bumps. Pulsing hot blood and desire. She could actually smell her own lust mingling with the citrus scent of her bath.

"Come in," *to my parlor, said the spider to the fly.*

With barely a foot inside the room, he scooped her up and kissed her thoroughly. She laughed and reciprocated. If she'd had the slightest doubt about the outcome of this evening—and she couldn't really recall one—it was gone before his lips touched hers a second time. She pressed herself close to him, gorged herself with the taste and smell of him, reveled in his touch.

She was killing him. She'd smiled her intent when she'd opened the door and now she was so pliant and giving in his arms, he was hard-pressed to control himself. Her mouth was a rare fine wine to be sipped and savored and yet he gulped like a rummy sailor, and it wasn't nearly enough to satisfy him. He left her gasping for air to deliver hot, searing kisses to her throat. The warm scent of her filled his head like a thick fog. She moaned, low and throaty, and trembled in his arms when his hand covered her breast. He whimpered at the painful pressure between his legs and forced himself to push her away.

"Ellen, Ellen," he said, panting as he shook his head, his forehead propped against hers. "Stop. You're killing me." He tried to relieve some of his tension with a laugh, but it was weak and ineffective. "It was a great idea, but I have to tell you, the timing stinks."

"The timing?" Timing? Granted, her mind was so muddled she barely recognized the word but . . . well, it seemed like a great time to her. "What timing?"

He took in a deep breath and let it out slowly. He still had his eyes closed and couldn't get the taste of her out of his mind.

"I want you so much. I . . . I'm crazy about you. I love you," he said, his hands gripping her upper arms, tighter every time he was tempted to reach out and undress her. "I think the very first time I saw you, I loved you."

And their timing stunk how?

"I know," she said breathlessly, her hand at his waist, drawing him toward her. "Well, I didn't know about you, how you felt at first, I mean . . . but I know now. And I think maybe I loved you, too, before I actually met you. I know I do now." She was babbling and he wasn't budging. She felt like a baby that someone was teasing with a pacifier, holding it close to her mouth then swooping it away, just out of reach. She curled her fingers through his belt loops and tugged a little harder. "I love you, Jonah."

He made a sobbing noise, then growled.

"Let's get this over with, then," he said, releasing her, taking a step back and shoving his hands deep in his pockets. He shook his head and smiled at her, almost as amused as he was frustrated.

First, his words had her pulling up short, hurt and bewildered. Get it over with? And then to stand there, looking at her expectantly . . . Tears stung her eyes as real, true anger rumbled in her stomach. Seductress and strumpet started with the same letter, but that's where the similarities ended in Ellen's book. She didn't like his attitude.

"What?" he asked, leaning forward to see her expression better. "Hey. It's not that I don't want to do this. I do. I was just hoping . . . well, I wasn't expecting to do it tonight, is all. I had other plans."

"We don't have to do it tonight," she said, seething. "We don't have to do it ever."

"No. No. I want to. I do."

"Forget it. You had other plans"—she waved a hand in the air—"go."

He frowned at her. He was missing some data.

"I'm supposed to go to dinner with your brother alone?" he asked, wondering if it was some weird midwestern courtship ritual he'd never heard of before. He'd do it if he had to, but he preferred to have her there.

"What?"

"Your brother?" He tipped his thumb behind him. "Felix? Down on the front porch, waiting for us?"

"What?" She stepped around him to look out the door and down the stairs.

"He's sitting on the front porch. He said you invited him to dinner tonight to meet me, to determine my intentions toward you."

"Your what?" She turned back to him even madder than before. "I'm going to kill him."

It didn't take an intelligence analyst to figure the situation out.

"Don't you dare laugh, Jonah. This isn't funny. Your intentions?" she sputtered.

"I know," he said, chuckling. "If he'd come up with me, he'd know my intentions."

"Oh. I really am going to kill him," she said, adding up her grievances. Impersonating a concerned brother. Spoiling her seduction. "Stop laughing. People always laugh and forgive him for just this sort of behavior and it makes me crazy."

"I'm sorry. It just seems like a very brotherly thing to do, any way you look at it."

"Well, he isn't going to get away with it this time," she said, grabbing her nightie-stuffed purse. "All he's getting to eat tonight is his teeth."

"Hey, hey, hey," he said, latching onto her wrist when she would have stormed out the door. "I don't really mind."

"Well, I do."

"I don't," he said again, soft and firm. "Because when dinner's over, you and I will have dessert alone."

How could she stay mad at him with a proposition like that on her plate?

"But you don't know Felix."

"Then this is as good a time as any to get to know him," he said, watching the war of emotions on her face. "I want to know your family. I want to know everything about you."

It was foolish to think she could hide Felix from him forever.

It did strange things to his insides to watch her give

in to her more generous nature. He loved that she couldn't hold on to a good mad for very long. He let go of her wrist to loop his arm around her waist. She was still a little stiff. He pressed a kiss to her temple, felt her go slack and lean against him. His lips moved into a smile against her hair, and he closed his eyes, deeply and profoundly happy.

"Spy stuff, huh?"

"Yeah, I guess so. Spy stuff," Jonah told Felix after the briefest hesitation. It was all in how you looked at it, he supposed. "It's more like playing with hidden picture puzzles and figuring out riddles. You see or . . . pick up on something different or out of place; you get curious; figure out what it is, why it's there, who done it." He grinned.

"Just like in the movies."

Jonah nodded, caught Ellen's eye, and smiled. "Except I don't sew things into the lining of my jackets or fold them into the heel of my shoes." He winked at her, and she twinkled back at him over the rim of her water glass.

He'd deliberately driven them by the junkyard on their way to the restaurant, curious to see her reaction. She'd been telling him an amusing anecdote about Felix's brief high school football career and hadn't skipped a beat, hadn't noticed the place at all in fact. But through his rearview mirror he would have sworn he saw her brother salute the place with his middle finger. He became curiouser and curiouser.

"Course not," Felix said, leaning forward to set his fresh glass of beer on the table, preparing to talk in earnest now. "But you make pretty good money, right?"

Evidently it had been too much to hope that he could act like a normal, healthy human being for the duration of a single meal. Still, she'd done exactly that—hoped. And she'd been pleased when he'd ordered beer instead of his usual Jack Daniels—until he started drinking it like water.

"Felix," she said, a warning in her voice. Both men glanced at her. One amused, the other a bit blurry-eyed.

"I make captain's wages. It's not too bad," Jonah told him, playing along with the concerned-brother act. He was in love with this guy's sister and would tell him anything he wanted to know, but he couldn't get over the feeling that there was more going on than a simple brotherly inquisition.

Ellen, though pleasant and chatty at the beginning of the meal, had become quiet, tense, and vigilant as her brother ordered beer after beer, his voice growing louder and louder, his gestures larger and more clumsy. Felix, on the other hand, in spite of his heavy drinking and the fact that he was sitting in the middle of a room full of people, appeared to be in hiding. He was watchful—of the front door, the people behind them, and the other customers' movements around the restaurant. He was jumpy, startling at the slightest noise, at the sudden appearance of a waiter, and frequently for no reason at all. And he was distracted, going through the motions of a routine getting-to-know-you conversation, showing no real interest—until now.

"But you're a single guy, never been married. You probably have a good bit stashed away. For a rainy day. A little nest egg."

"Some," he said, nodding.

"Felix. This isn't any of your business."

"It is if he plans to marry my sister." He tipped his glass back and poured the second half of the amber fluid down his throat. Licking his lips, he added, "With Dad gone, it's up to me to make sure her future is . . . uh . . . um . . ."

"Secure?" Jonah suggested helpfully.

"Yes. Exactly. Secure."

"Felix." For pity's sake, she hadn't managed to seduce him yet, much less get a marriage proposal. "That's enough. You wanted to meet him, you've met him. His personal life, and especially his finances, aren't your concern."

"They are if he plans to—"

"We've known each other less than a week," she said, hurrying to cut him off before he said it again. "*We* haven't even discussed marriage." Her gaze snagged Jonah's. "Yet."

He grinned at her and leaned back in his chair, lacing his fingers together, thumbs propped pad to pad as he watched her. She was suddenly too warm and felt like squirming in her chair. He didn't appear particularly sensitive to the subject; looked pleased even that she'd added that last word.

Felix, looking from one to the other with a drunken astuteness, rolled his eyes.

"I need another beer."

"Try the water," she suggested, reluctantly tearing her eyes from Jonah's. "You haven't asked about Jonah's father yet."

"I don't know his father," he muttered, then recalling his role, he came up with, "Oh. The bloodline.

Right." He wagged his finger at her, then at Jonah. "You got any nuts in your tree?"

Her eyes closed slowly as she heard Jonah laugh.

"I don't think so," he said, chuckling. "What about you? Anything I should know about your family gene pool?"

Her eyes popped open again. If he was referring to alcoholism, he was doing so casually and with great good humor.

Felix thought about it while he waved to get the waitress's attention for another drink. "I always thought Uncle Lou was a weird fish. Didn't you, El? You did, I remember." To Jonah, he said, "Elly used to think he was possessed by the devil because no dog would approach him. He'd call to them and they'd run the other way. Throw sticks for them, and they'd just keep on running. But I think that was because he smelled bad. That guy used to eat cloves of garlic like they were chocolates. Remember that, Elly?"

She nodded. She could have brought up his disease then, laid it out on the table. If Jonah hadn't guessed at it yet, she was pretty sure he wouldn't be appalled by it. Maybe the three of them could discuss it? Maybe he could help? Maybe . . . maybe another time, she thought, her courage losing out to a deep-seated, irrational shame she had no control over.

"Course, he was my dad's uncle by marriage, I think," Felix was saying, his mind clearly befuddled. "You wouldn't have to worry about the garlic thing unless you were planning to marry my cousin Dotty. Now, there's a weird one. . . ."

"Felix," she said, quietly. "That's not what I meant. I meant that Jonah's father has been ill and you haven't asked how he is yet. It would be polite."

"Oh. Well, I didn't know he was sick," he said, though he'd been told several times earlier in the conversation. He looked at Jonah. "How's your dad?"

Jonah reached out to toy with an unused dinner knife. "No different. He's had a stroke," he said for Felix's re-edification. He looked at Ellen. "But more interesting."

She'd been waiting all night to hear about Earl's mysterious lady. She perked up instantly, forgetting Felix even existed. That didn't seem a difficult task for Jonah either, as he spoke directly to her.

"More human, I guess."

"Tell me," she said, leaning forward. "Mr. Gunther's daughter-in-law, what's she like? What did she say?"

He met her halfway across the table, the tips of his fingers instinctively seeking hers to create a connection between them.

"She didn't know what to say at first. She didn't know I was here," he said, then added, "But she knew who I was."

Ellen grinned. She could tell it meant the earth and stars to him to know his father had claimed him, even in some small way, as his son. That the woman knew he existed was all the proof he needed.

"She lives on a small nonworking farm outside town. She's planning to move though. Two of her three children are grown and gone and the third is finishing college, and the place is too big for her to handle alone." He shrugged. That was neither here nor there, but he had to start somewhere, right? "A real nice lady. She said she'd only spoken to my father a couple of times in person, but that she'd owed him such a huge debt for so long that she felt like she'd known him for most of her life."

"Because he saved her husband's life."

He nodded. "They'd just gotten married when he left for Vietnam. No children till after the war." He could see she understood the significance in that. "We went down to the hospital cafeteria and had coffee. She told me the whole story."

She didn't have to ask him to repeat the story for her. He could have told the whole world, he was so happy to know it, but she was the one he wanted to tell first. So, in a voice that Felix could listen to—or not— he told her the only solid, personal history he knew about his father.

Just as Denise Gunther had, he painted a picture of a war-torn Asian country where it was often impossible to tell friend from foe among the natives; where hit- and-run jungle tactics and twenty-one ruthless years of war experience by the opposition had American soldiers feeling overly wary and distrustful, and at a distinct dis- advantage. A place where a cry for help could just as easily be an invitation to death, and everyone knew it. According to her, her husband had barely noticed the photographer attached to his squad. Though the group was small, with only seven men left, the photographer had been older, a quiet sort who kept to himself. He took his pictures without getting in anyone's way and, in general, blended with the jungle and carnage as if he were invisible.

"Which explains how he could get the shots he did," Jonah said, thinking of the awards and plaques on his father's living room wall and all he'd gone through to get them. He imagined there was an incredible story behind each and every one of them. "He had to have been right in the middle of it to get them."

She could see he was still processing much of it in his mind, arranging it on his personal timeline, maybe realizing how close he'd come to never knowing his father at all, or maybe ever being born.

"What year was this?"

"Nineteen sixty-nine. I wasn't even a year old."

Silently she waited for him to continue.

Trying to maintain an emotional detachment from an event that had happened to a near stranger while he was still in his infancy made the rest of the story relatively easy to tell. Naturally, Mrs. Gunther knew her husband's side of the story better than she knew Earl Blake's. She'd related his account of a routine patrol through a town that had recently undergone heavy mortar bombing. The squad had been met with smoldering rubble and debris, burnt-out buildings and, as was often the case, a sniper ambush. She'd been vague about the details but seemed to recall her husband's horror as vividly as if he were telling the story himself— or as if she'd heard about it enough times to know it that well.

Just before dusk on that hot, humid day in Vietnam, Levy Gunther, Jr., the only son of a camera shop owner in Quincey, Indiana, had taken a sniper bullet through his right leg, the pain blazing through his body and exploding in his head. And while the rest of his squad had scattered and shot blindly in the direction of the following shots, he'd thrashed about in plain sight, taking a second shot in his right shoulder.

He screamed, felt his world go black, heard a voice whispering. . . .

"Don't . . . move . . . a muscle." He'd heard the

whisper through the gunfire, the angry, desperate shouting of his buddies, and his own pain. *"Don't . . . move . . . a muscle. Don't make a sound. Be dead."* He was howling in pain and fear—but only in his mind. Somehow, some way, the whisper had reached him, sure and commanding, and he had obeyed it. *"Be dead. They won't waste another bullet on you if they think you're dead."* Time passed, eons it seemed, but the whisper remained, constant and comforting. *"I can see you're still breathing. I know you're not dead. I won't leave you. I won't leave you. . . ."*

"Jeez," Felix muttered, hanging over his beer glass in rapt attention.

Ellen shook off the chills racing up and down her spine and looked at him, then back to Jonah, who seemed to be watching their reactions closely. It gratified him to see that he wasn't the only one to react emotionally to the story, not the only one to think of his father as a hero.

"So, I guess he bled to death, huh?"

"Felix!" She sighed loudly and Jonah laughed. "He lived to tell the story and father three children."

They could almost hear the memory tape rewinding in his head. "Oh, yeah. Right. Your dad . . . he must have been the whisperer, then."

Jonah nodded, smiling. "He stayed hidden behind a pile of rubble, waited for dark and for things to quiet down. Then he picked up Gunther and carried him back to the aid station and disappeared. Mrs. Gunther said it wasn't until her husband came home and saw himself in one of the photos that he even knew my father's name. She said they wrote to him dozens of times to thank him, but he never answered. Her husband later died in a car accident. I guess he had a bad time, nightmares . . . flashbacks."

The three of them were silent for a moment, each in their own way marveling over the workings of the human spirit; feeling pride and yet wondering at it's insanity; questioning their own grit.

"Did your old man get a medal or something for saving that guy?" Felix asked.

He shook his head. "I don't think so. I don't think anyone but the Gunthers knew about it or thought of it as anything out of the ordinary. She said that the few times she visited him, after he moved here, he asked her not to talk about it. Said he could barely remember the incident, like it was all in a day's work."

"Maybe it was," she said. "To him. Lots of things happen in a war."

Jonah's brows rose, and he nodded his acquiescence. "He never could figure out why they'd left the house and shop to him, I guess. He told her that he thought Levy Gunther was some distant relative he'd never met or heard of, that he hadn't known what to do with the property when he'd inherited it, so he didn't do anything with it. Just tossed the papers in a drawer."

"I guess you didn't inherit your curiosity from him," Felix observed mildly, his eyelids drooping.

"I guess not," he said, thinking of several other personality traits that they might not share, if Denise Gunther's description of his father was accurate. "She said he was eccentric."

"Eccentric? How?" Ellen asked, noting from the tone of his voice that eccentric wasn't what he would have called him.

He lifted one shoulder uncertainly. "Introverted, she said. Not shy, not a recluse, because he came and went at will and spoke his mind when he felt like it, but was happier in his own company than he was in the company of others. He wouldn't allow anyone to get involved in his life, didn't get involved in theirs. Was polite but not forthcoming. She said she visited several times and finally stopped when it became obvious he didn't care one way or the other. After that, her gratitude turned to a sense of responsibility, I guess. She'd drive by the shop three or four times a week to make sure it was open, and that he was doing okay, but stopped intruding on his life."

"Intruding? That's the word she used?"

He nodded, recalling it clearly. "I suppose that's how he made her feel."

She mulled this over, then asked, "But then, how did she know about you?"

"I asked her that same thing," he said, shifting his weight as he got to the best part of the story. "On her second or third visit to the house, they were sitting together in the living room in silence. Just sitting there. She said she was feeling very uncomfortable and he was reading something in the newspaper as if she weren't even there. She was just about to make an excuse and leave when he folded up the paper and announced he was going to show her a picture of his son."

Felix laughed. "No offense, but that guy doesn't sound like he had all his dogs barkin'."

"Felix!" She threw him a derisive glare, then looked back at Jonah. "Why? Had he read something about you in the paper?"

He shook his head. "I don't think so. I don't know. He just stood up and opened his wallet and showed her an old baby picture of me. Then he told her all about me. Everything. About how I spent my vacations at boarding school and my career and where I was stationed now and that I was a loner like him."

"A loner?"

"That I lived alone. Had few close friends. Ate alone in restaurants . . ."

"Man, it doesn't sound like you got all your dogs barkin' either," Felix said. "A guy like you. Makes good money. Stand-up job. Women oughtta be crawlin' all over you. Whatsa matter with you?" He looked to Ellen for a hint, saw the look on her face. "Well, nothin', I guess, 'cuz my sister is!" Then he laughed at his own pathetic joke.

Cringing with shame and flushed with embarrassment, she watched him wave to the waitress again.

"No more, Felix. You've had enough. And I've had enough of you. It's time to go," she said quietly, sending an imploring, apologetic glance to Jonah. His smile was small and reassuring, but it didn't make her feel any better.

They gathered their belongings, paid the bill, and rode most of the way back to Ellen's apartment in a stiff silence that Ellen controlled. She started it and she'd have to break it—even Felix was wise enough to know that. She had things to say to both men, things that neither was in a hurry to hear—one fearing the pain it would cause her, the other afraid of the pain it would cause him.

"So," she said finally, opting to avoid both conversations. "Do you think your father had you investigated?"

"I don't know," Jonah said with a quick glance to judge her mood. "Maybe. But an investigator might have taken more pictures, and the only one I've been able to find is the one in his wallet."

She smiled then. "It was there?"

"Yes," he said, smiling too. "In his wallet in his bed-side table. It's old and faded and frayed, but it's there."

"Any other pictures? Of other people?"

He shook his head slowly.

She reached out and touched his arm, leaned toward him a little. In a voice that was brimming with emotion, she said softly, "He cared, Jonah."

CHAPTER EIGHT

STEP EIGHT

*Even if you're on the right track, you'll get run
over if you sit there long enough.*
—Will Rogers

*Always a day late and a dollar short? Maybe there's a
reason for that. If your plan is logical, practical, and
doable, why put it off? All the good intentions in the
world can't accomplish as much as one good action.
Delay, and you give the situation time to change. Pro-
crastinate, and you may be too late . . . once again.*

"You're going."
"I'm not."
"You're going."
"He'll kill me."
"You're going or I'll kill you."
Dry breakfast cereal with Felix was a poor substitute
for the postseduction repast she'd planned the day be-
fore, and she wasn't above displaying some of her re-

sentment. While his showing up for dinner hadn't necessarily precluded the eventual employment of the teal blue negligee, his behavior during the meal had certainly put a damper on it. When he'd loudly refused to be dropped off at his apartment, and then sullenly acquiesced to being taken to his mother's house for the night—in spite of his roundly stated qualms about waking her up and causing her to worry—he'd thrown the whole idea into the deep freeze.

She'd stood on the front porch with Jonah, feeling not the euphoria she'd anticipated, but utter mortification.

"He has a drinking problem," she'd said.

"I noticed."

"It's hereditary."

"So are a million other diseases."

If she hadn't loved him before, his quiet acceptance and gentle understanding would have put her over the top. That and his empathy for the shame she felt for something she had no control over.

"My dad had it too."

"Funny how you can hate something about someone you love so much, isn't it?"

Funny, too, how the long embrace they'd shared had seemed even more satisfying somehow than wild, passionate sex might have at that moment.

Now she told Felix, "I'm dropping you off at Mom's and she's going to baby-sit you until I come back for you at five-thirty. Then I'm personally driving you over to Krane's, and you're going to take the job he offers you and pay him back every cent you owe him. You can't put this off any longer, Felix. You have to settle things with Mr. Krane. And this is the perfect opportunity. He's willing to give you a job and you're going to take it. Finish your coffee."

He sighed and rubbed both his hands over his face, pushing his blond hair out of his bloodshot eyes. "It doesn't work that way, Ellen," he said, doing his best to reason with her. "If Krane were willing to give jobs to everyone who owed him money and couldn't pay him back, do you think it would still look like a dump?" He pushed his coffee cup away. "He's not running some welfare project over there. This isn't give-a-bum-a-job week. There's a reason there's just the two of them working there."

She looked at him and when it became apparent that she was waiting to hear the reason, he rolled his eyes and spread his arms out wide. "He doesn't want employees. He wants his money."

"Then why would he agree to hire you?" She was down to her last ounce of patience with him when she reached out and put a hand on his arm, trying to reassure him. "I admit, he's a creepy looking guy, but once I explained the situation to him and pointed out that some money was better than no money, he was very reasonable about the whole thing. Now, he might not pay you a lot, minimum wage, so you might want to think about moving in with Mom for a while. Just until you get him paid off. And you've got to stop drinking, Felix."

"That's easy for you to say."

She sighed. "I know. I do. I know. But you've got to get some help. I can't help you. I wish I could, but I can't. You have to help yourself. And you're just going to go from one mess to another if you don't put a stop to it." She paused to let that sink in. "This is the first step, Felix. This is the right thing to do. Stand up and take responsibility for yourself. Pay your debt to Mr. Krane. Get some help. Just, for once in your life, do the right thing."

"Or?" he said, hearing the desperation in her voice.

"Or . . ." she said, only half believing she'd be able to back up her words and knowing everything would get worse if she didn't. "Or I'll wash my hands of you. I will. And I mean it this time. I'll make sure Mom and Jane do too. You won't have anyone left who will have anything to do with you."

Her heart wept as she sat and looked him straight in the eye, calling his bluff. Neither one of them were good gamblers, she was afraid. Her poker face felt cold and unnatural, but she wouldn't let it slip. There was too much at stake. He was too much to lose.

Finally she watched as disbelief gave way to uncertainty, as doubt gave way to humble despair.

"It's not going to work. I'll screw it up. You know that," he said, resigned. "But I'll give it a try."

"Good," she said, patting his arm and giving it a gentle, loving squeeze. "Good." She stood up from the table, half afraid she'd cry, not wanting to make too big a deal of the hope spewing forth inside her. "Maybe Mom can take you over and get your hair cut today and—"

"Don't push it, Ellen." He glowered at her.

She held up both hands. "One step at a time." She picked up their breakfast dishes and started off to the kitchen sink. "Don't forget, now. Five-thirty. We don't want to be late."

"I'll go by myself."

She wanted to let him go by himself. He was a grown man, he should go by himself. She didn't really relish the idea of going back to that junkyard. But the simple truth was, she didn't trust him.

"No. I'm driving you there. Don't bother to argue with me. I've made up my mind."

He didn't bother, but when she emerged from the kitchen, he was waiting for her, a frown on his face.

"Are you all right?" he asked. "You've been acting weird lately."

Weird or confident? she wanted to ask. If Felix, through his dazed view of the world, had noticed the change in her, then the little green book was truly working. She smiled. But explaining the little green book to Felix *would* have been weird, so she just said, "I'm fine."

"Must be that guy from last night that's making you act so different."

"Jonah. His name is Jonah." And just the thought of him set her world right.

"I know." A pause. "I liked him."

He was such a baby sometimes that it was hard to remember he was still a man, still thought of himself as the man in the family—that deep down inside he might have enough pride left to believe his opinion counted.

She smiled at him, then swooped down to plant a kiss on his cheek. "Thanks, Felix," she said softly near his ear. "I'm glad you like him. What you think is important to me." She stood up straight. "Now bag up the trash for me and set it outside the door for Eugene, will you? I have to finish getting ready."

She was the teeniest, tiniest, weeniest bit late for work that morning, but certainly not late enough to be attracting looks throughout the day.

Too-nice people weren't accustomed to being looked at, to feeling paranoid. Who'd want to persecute a really nice person? Who'd be out to get one? Trusting other people to be nice was part of the too-nice complex. So perhaps the new, not-so-nice Ellen was over-reacting to something she'd never noticed before—at least that's what she was hoping as she looked up once again and caught two tellers talking, looking at her, then suddenly looking away.

Maybe she'd only imagined Mary Westford's and Sylvia Plant's voices through the restroom door; maybe they hadn't gone suddenly silent when she walked in; maybe their reaction to her wasn't a whole season colder than usual. Maybe this was how people normally acted and she was just now noticing. Or maybe something was wrong.

"Vi," she whispered in her over-the-divider voice.

"What?"

"Have you noticed anything strange or different around here?"

"You mean other than you?"

She smiled, glad that Vi had noticed the changes in her too. But the changes she'd made were for the better; they weren't that strange and they weren't that different.

"Yes. Other than me."

"Nope."

She sighed. Maybe it was her imagination. . . .

Joleen didn't mention that she'd noticed anything out of the ordinary when they talked in her office just before the bank closed for the day.

"I know you asked to leave a bit early today, Ellen, and that's fine, I won't keep you. I just wanted to make sure you hadn't changed your mind about taking Mary

Westford's position while she's on leave. Do you still want the job?"

That was never the issue. Wanting the job. She was very happy with the job she had. "I deserve that promotion, don't I?"

"Yes, of course you do."

"Then I want it."

It was a good thing she and Jonah had agreed to meet later at the hospital—so he could visit with his father while she took care of some family business—because she left work feeling testy and out of sorts. Jumpy. Nervous. Maybe Felix and the job at Krane's had affected her whole day at the bank, without her even realizing it. Maybe his paranoia was rubbing off on her.

There wasn't an ounce of rational thinking to her hurrying home to change from skirt to slacks before she picked up Felix. Her reaction to some deep-seated and inconsistent concept about a skirt in a junkyard was easier to comply with than to argue with, she supposed. But to save time, she parked out in front of the house, dashing up the sidewalk, across the porch, and in through the front door.

"Ellen," Mrs. Phipps said, startled as they met in the hallway. "You're home early. We were just about to—"

"Not today, Mrs Phipps," she said, rushing up the stairs with hardly a pause. She frowned at the trash bag still sitting outside her apartment door. Had she gotten the day confused? No. It was Thursday, trash day. "Shoot," she said, jamming the key in the lock and letting herself in.

Fat Bubba had followed her up the stairs. He loitered in the doorway a fraction of a second too long.

"Not today, Bubba," she said, using the same hurried, impersonal tone of voice she'd used on Mrs. Phipps as she swung the door closed on him.

Fifteen minutes later she was in jeans and a white T-shirt, out the front door, and heading for her car. She had the eerie feeling someone was watching her and turned to wave good-bye to Mrs. Phipps, but the old lady wasn't standing in her window and Eugene's shades were drawn. She slowed down for a second, noticing that the house looked older than usual somehow, and sad in a way she couldn't define. And worse, with the shades drawn and the curtains closed against the summer sun, it was almost as if it were shutting her out, turning its back on her—which was ridiculous, of course.

She shook off a peculiar sensation of foreboding and got into her car. On the way to her mother's house she tried to get enthusiastic about what she was doing, but deep inside a dark, misty fog of uneasiness churned and swirled. As right and as bright as the day before had been, this day was filled with dark suspicions and apprehension, and she didn't know why.

But for Felix's sake she was smiling when she honked the horn outside her mother's house and waved cheerfully to them both when they stepped out onto the front porch. Surprisingly, he jogged down the walk and quickly got into the car.

"Go. Quick," he said, slamming the door closed. "Hurry, before she puts more spit in my hair."

Laughing, she complied. That their mother had had a field day dressing her son for a job interview was too obvious. His old short-sleeved cotton shirt was patched and pressed, his T-shirt was bright white, and there was a razor-sharp crease down each leg of his ragged jeans. Even his tennis shoes had a fresh coat of powdery white polish on them. He was shaved and his hair was clean and combed—and apparently held in place with Super Hold Spit.

"Big day for Mom, huh?"

"The first day of school revisited," he said, letting loose a huge sigh as he started to relax a bit. "All I need is a backpack and some lunch money." She chuckled, and he glared at her. "Sure, laugh. But it's a sad day when a grown man actually runs toward his own death just to get away from his mother, you know."

"Oh, stop," she said, scoffing. "You haven't looked this good in months, number one. And number two, you're not running to your death. You're taking your first step toward a new life. You're doing what's right. You're taking responsibility for yourself, and I happen to be very proud of you."

"Great. That makes all the difference to me," he said in a sarcastic tone of voice. However, she noticed that he squirmed in his seat a bit and sat up a little straighter, smoothed out the creases in his jeans. "I'll keep that in mind during my recuperation."

"I'm serious," she said, knowing that he knew she was, but wanting to pump up his ego a bit more. "What you're doing takes a lot of guts, Felix. Facing Krane like this, attempting to pay back your debt. I'm proud to call you my brother."

She waited for his next quip, but when it didn't come and the silence changed into something palpable, she glanced at him, found him pale and serious and regarding her with great affection.

"I haven't been much of a brother to you lately,

have I?" he asked, and before she could deny the re-mark, he said, "You know, if anything happens today, if something goes wrong, I want you to know that you've been a good sister to me. You get mad sometimes, but you've never turned your back on me and I . . . I ap-preciate that."

"Felix."

"I know I'm a pain in the ass. I know people have told you to have nothing to do with me. To practice tough love on me."

"And I did," she said defensively. "I do. Because I think they're right. And look how well it's worked. You're standing up for yourself. You're—"

"You tried. But you never once left me to sleep out in the cold or go hungry. You never turned your back on me."

"Well, no." If she had, this day of reckoning might have come years earlier, but being a too-nice person sort of precluded letting your brother starve or freeze to death. Another fine demonstration of the fact that being too nice wasn't the best thing to be. "No, I didn't. And I'm sorry for that. Maybe if I had—"

"This day would have come sooner?" he asked, fin-ishing her sentence for her. His laugh was hollow. "This day wouldn't have come at all, Elly. I'd be dead by now." She opened her mouth to deny it, to cham-pion his will to live and the common sense he had when he wasn't drinking, but he stopped her. "I just want you to know that you've been a good sister and I love you."

Tears pressed hard on the backs of her eyes and stung to make them water. Good sister, bad sister wasn't really important now. They'd hit the crux of their conversation. "I love you, too, Felix."

There was a new kind of kinship between them as

they pulled up across the street from the junkyard. There was a silent mutual agreement that if Felix was going to stand up like a man, he was also to be treated like one—and neither one was too sure Krane would feel the same.

"Okay," she said, turning her head to face him. "Tonight he's just going to show you around, discuss wages and the terms of the pay-back agreement, and then you start work tomorrow, so this shouldn't take too long. I'll wait right here for you. If you're not back in thirty minutes, I'm coming in after you. Okay?"

He nodded, but the look in his eyes told her that he suspected Krane could inflict a great deal of pain in thirty minutes.

"Twenty minutes," she said, forcing the fear from her voice. "Twenty minutes and I'm coming in. How long does it take to look around a junkyard anyway, huh?"

"Stay in the car, Elly," he said, his tone flat and reconciled. "I can handle this."

"Twenty minutes and I'm coming in."

His gaze slipped from the door of the run-down building across the street to meet hers. He'd told her to stay in the car, but he couldn't bring himself to forbid her to follow him. He tried to smile, but the gesture held no reassurance for her that he thought anything other than that he was going to see his Maker.

"Everything is going to be fine," she said, falling back on her assumption that all people were basically good.

Once more he nodded. He took a deep breath and pulled on the door handle to get out. He walked slowly across the street and through the dusty parking lot. It was 5:40 and there was still plenty of daylight, though an evening dullness had taken most of the blazing glare from it, so she could see him perfectly. His one look back was quick, an afterthought to his turning the knob to go in. He was scared.

Ellen fidgeted, chewed her lower lip, and watched the clock in her dashboard blink off each second. At 5:43 she pulled on the handle of the car door and got out. She started across the street, then turned around and went back to lean against her car. If things were going well in there, the last thing Felix needed was his big sister barging in to hold his hand as if he were a baby.

Still, with every minute that passed, she became more and more certain that she'd made a huge mistake; that for the first time in Felix's life he might be right about something. She should go over there, she thought. So what if she embarrassed Felix? They'd think she was the reason for his drinking. She could pull a dumb-female trick: "Can I join the tour, pretty please? I've never seen a real junkyard before," she could say.

She turned to look at the clock and at the same time heard the door across the street squeak open.

The burly man from the rusty stool came out first, then Felix, followed by Tom Krane. Her heart was thumping out a funeral cadence, slow, loud, and resounding. In a bizarre, almost dreamlike moment their steps matched the slow, solemn thumping as they walked to the side of the building and the open gate of a tall wire fence. She noticed she was holding her breath when Felix looked over at her, and she didn't release it when he smiled and waved.

"You better go on home, Ellen," he shouted to her, his companions slowing and turning their heads to watch. "This is going to take longer than we thought. It may be a while. You go on home, and I'll bum a ride home from one of them."

She frowned, tried to see his face more clearly, tried to pick up a signal in his voice that something was wrong. He smiled and waved again, then turned back and fell into step with the other two men, saying, "Thanks for the ride over here. I'll see you later." Fifteen more slow plodding steps, and he disappeared through the fence and behind a pile of junk. Her heart was about to burst. She let go of the stale air in her lungs and took a deep breath. She must have needed the extra oxygen, because it seemed to snap and fizz inside her brain, shake things loose, help her see things more clearly.

Or not . . .

She wasn't really sure what set her off or why. She just knew, with every fiber of her being, that something was wrong. Horribly wrong. And she was running. *They're not going to give him a lift home. Why would they give him a lift home? These are not nice men; they wouldn't give their grandmother a ride home.* Over and over in her mind the alarms went off on a sour note. She thought she heard her name being called, thought it was Felix calling her. The fear was disorienting her though, the call seemed to come from behind and it didn't sound like Felix's voice. But she knew it was him and kept running, through the gate in the wire fence.

But once inside, she had to stop. The junkyard was much bigger than it looked from across the street. There were three primary avenues, one straight ahead and one off to each side from where she stood. Cars and car parts were piled two and three deep along each side of the avenues—buses, bikes, and baby carriages dispersed among them. Refrigerators and metal rowboats; tractors and trailers. There were acres of them. She moved forward a bit to where the three roads intersected, looking down each, catching a movement off to the right—about a hundred feet down.

Coming up on the spot, she heard a muffled cry, then in a small alcove of debris she saw Burlyman grab hold of Felix, and Krane deliver a crushing blow to his face.

"No! No!" she screamed, watching blood splatter and ooze from her brother's nose and mouth. The burly man did something to Felix's arm, and he cried out in pain. "No!"

With the instant recognition that her words weren't going to stop them, she took a running start, grimaced at the next blow to Felix's midsection, took a flying jump, and landed on Krane's back. His arm came up to throw her off and she wrapped her leg around it. With both arms firmly around his neck—and not daring to let go—she could smell the grease and sweat and pure evil on him. Instinctively curling her lips back to avoid contact with him, she sank her teeth into the fleshy part of his shoulder at the base of his neck.

He howled and bucked like a crazed bronc. She felt his skin give way under the pressure of her teeth, tasted blood in her mouth. Then she was flying. . . .

Everything after that happened in a blur. First she was whizzing through the air, then it felt as if she were shattering into a thousand little pieces as she came crashing down to the ground, hitting the side of an old panel truck, her head knocking it twice before the world tunneled in and out of focus. In and out, and while she fought the hazy darkness she was aware of the noise. Lots of voices, lots of shouting—more than the three men she knew to be in the junkyard with her. Panic gripped her as she remembered Felix, his face bloody and broken. Were lots of men attacking him now? She was desperate to see.

"Felix?" she cried out, the fog turning gray and beginning to thin out. Fuzzy shapes and forms crossed her field of vision. Khaki uniforms. Lots of them. "Felix?"

"He'll be okay," someone beside her said. She turned her head and blinked her eyes until she had a clear picture of Bobby Ingles. Thank God she'd been too nice to be cruel to him in school. He was watching the six or seven other police officers crowded around Felix and the two loan sharks, when he said, "Looks like he's beat up a bit, but he'll be okay. He knew he might have to take a couple hits before we could get in here."

"He what? He knew what?" Supporting herself on one elbow, she rolled forward onto her hands and knees to get up. Every muscle in her body felt as if it had been pinched, viciously. "He knew what?"

"That he might have to take a couple punches before we could get in here to arrest those two."

Using the panel truck to guide her, and Bobby's hand for support, she stood up and scowled at him through the dizziness in her head. "What the hell are you talking about?" She took a tentative step toward the huddle around her brother and winced with pain. The next step was just as bad, but the one after that was a little better. Talking helped. "Felix didn't know this was going to happen. I made him come here. I almost got him killed."

"He suspected. We all did," Bobby said, following her at a discreet distance when it became apparent that she didn't want or need his help to walk. "Especially after the other night at the hospital."

She was vaguely aware of the ambulance pulling into the back of the junkyard, advancing toward them. She needed to get to Felix. She hobbled a little faster.

"I don't understand, Bobby. I don't understand any of this. I understand that I was a fool, but the rest . . . I just don't understand."

"Tuesday night at the hospital—" he began, but she'd caught a glimpse of her brother and started pushing people away to get to him.

"Aw, Felix, Felix," she cried, kneeling down beside his battered body, his face swelling and discoloring under the blood. So much blood. "I'm so sorry. I'm so, so sorry." Tears rolled freely down her cheeks. "Can you see me? Can you hear me? Felix?" Only his left eye was swollen closed; he opened the right one and glanced around trying to find her. "I'm here, Felix. I'm sorry. Please be all right." He tried to speak, tried to wet his lips with a bloodied tongue, and the pain twisted his face. "Don't talk. Don't talk. He needs help. Someone help him. Don't die, Felix. Please don't die."

She wasn't sure what drew her attention to it— through the tears and anguish and hubbub going on around them—but she suddenly felt his fingers grasping hers, squeezing them tight, shaking them a bit, like a victorious combatant.

"That's right. That's right, Felix," she said, brushing away her tears with the back of her hand and trying to smile at him. "You won. You were right all along. I don't know how you did all this, but you won."

"Any time Krane's name comes up, we know something's going down. Tuesday night when Felix was trying so hard to get himself arrested, taken into custody so Krane couldn't get at him, I figured he was in some sort of trouble," Bobby Ingles said. He sat across from her in the surgical waiting room, speaking softly, calmly—explaining what had transpired that evening. His hands were clasped between his knees and he was leaning forward on his elbows. Felix had been wheeled into surgery twenty minutes earlier. "Between the time Felix sobered up and the time your mother came to pick him up, we asked him about the situation. He denied over and over again that he was in trouble with Krane. He said he knew who Krane was but had no personal relationship with the man. I told him then what Krane was like." He spread his fingers wide, helpless. "I told him he wasn't the first guy to get in a bind with him and he wouldn't be the last guy we found beaten half to death in a gutter somewhere."

"If you knew Krane was loan-sharking and beating up people, why didn't you arrest him?"

"No proof. And his victims were too afraid to testify against him."

"I don't understand that," she said, bewildered. "They can't pay him if they're too beaten up to work. It still doesn't make sense."

"Power," he said simply. "They beat up one person and everyone else moves heaven and earth to pay him. It generates fear."

"And they were going to use Felix to teach—"

A movement in the doorway caught her attention; she looked up. There stood Jonah, a safe haven, a light in the darkness, a warm bed on a cold night. There stood Jonah, vital, sexy, and all male.

It was as if someone pulled her plug and let all the air out of her, or as if she'd been holding herself together with paper clips and chewing gum while she waited for him—and now that he was there, she could fall apart and he'd pick up all the pieces.

Without a word from either of them, she stood and walked straight into his embrace.

He held her, rocking her gently, feeling an overwhelming gratitude for he knew not what.

He moved his hand from her back to the side of her head, to hold her close. She cringed.

"What? Are you hurt? I saw them bring Felix in from upstairs, then you arrived in the cop car. Are you hurt?" He held her away to check for himself. There were bruises, on her arms and legs, and a few minor scratches. "They wouldn't let me in to see you and then they said you were over here, that Felix was in surgery. Ellen, what's happened?"

"I'm fine," she said, palming his cheek to ease his concern. "I banged my head, but I'm fine. Felix is in surgery. He has a broken nose and mandible, a fractured arm, and some cracked ribs." She shook her head. "It's all my fault."

"Were you in an accident?"

"No, no, nothing like that. I wish we had been," she said, taking his hand as she turned back to Bobby Ingles. She made introductions and gave a brief explanation of what she knew. "Felix told me they'd kill him, but I didn't believe him. I made him go and now . . ." She held out her hands to show that she'd gotten Felix worse than nothing by making him go.

"Actually, that worked out pretty well," Bobby said, picking up the tale. "On Wednesday, when your mother told him you'd gone to Krane and gotten him a job, Felix must have figured he was going to lose this one, one way or another. With you or with Krane. So he called me. I'd told him that morning that if he was willing to wear a wire and testify against Krane, we could put the guy away for a good long while. Shut down his operation. Felix called that afternoon and said he would."

"But we had dinner with him that night," she said, glancing at Jonah for confirmation. "He didn't say a word about it."

"He couldn't. Krane isn't stupid and he knew we were onto him. One slip and we'd have him. The way you interceded for Felix was a perfect setup, and Felix said if you knew the truth you'd never let him go."

"Well, of course I wouldn't have. Walking in there like that was suicidal. What I did was stupid, but what he did was—"

"Pretty gutsy, if you ask me," Bobby said. "He actually planned most of it himself. Told us to come wire him up in your mother's backyard while your mother was inside taking her afternoon nap. Told us we had to let you drive him over, so that Krane wouldn't get suspicious. But you had to leave before we could do anything. That waving and telling you to go home was our signal that things were going sour, that Krane had no intention of giving him a job. And it was perfect except . . ."

"Except that I didn't leave on cue," she said, not too sure how she was feeling anymore. She didn't know if Felix was just plain stupid or brave beyond her dreams. Krane's arrest was a good thing, but she wasn't too sure the price Felix had paid was worth it. She was only half mad that no one had told her the plan—the other half understood completely.

One thing she *was* sure of was that if she hadn't been so puffed up with attitude, if she hadn't thought herself all powerful and capable of handling Felix's affairs without any help from anyone else, if she hadn't been so impatient to have *her* life the way *she* wanted it—including a quick cure for Felix—none of this would have happened.

"No, you didn't leave on cue," Bobby said, standing to leave. "But if you had, Krane wouldn't have that huge hole in his neck." He grinned at her. "Cops can't do that sort of thing, but we sure do enjoy it when someone else does it."

Jonah passed her a confused frown, and she shook her head indicating she'd explain it later. He watched her stand and offer a friendly hand to the officer and thank him. She looked exhausted, but beyond that she was remarkable. Bobby Ingles's story filled in most of the pieces to his puzzle. He thought of the courage it had taken for her to go to the junkyard in her brother's name, to face down men like that to protect him. He couldn't help wishing to know that kind of love someday.

Before Ingles could make a clean getaway, Ellen's mother and sister and brother-in-law arrived in an anxious, confused state. Ellen told them what had happened, and while the young police officer filled in the blanks and answered their questions, she turned back to Jonah. She came to sit beside him and, sliding her arm between his and his rib cage, lowered her head to his shoulder with a sigh.

"I'm so glad you're here," she said, closing her eyes, taking in the clean masculine smell of him, feeling the warmth of his body seeping into hers through two thin layers of cloth. "Where did you come from?"

He sensed she didn't mean it literally and gave her a squeeze. "Do you want to stay until Felix is out of surgery or can I take you home? You look exhausted."

"I am," she said, feeling it in every inch of muscle she possessed. She didn't know if her brain was a muscle, but she was feeling it there too. Every effort to think was painful and aborted for a limbo where she didn't have to bend over backward trying to decide if what she'd done—what she'd forced Felix into—was a good thing or bad, if her motive was selfish or sisterly, or if she could live with what she discovered. "I really am. But Mom and Jane want to meet you, and I should hang around to make sure Felix is okay."

"How about I meet Mom and Jane, briefly, and they call you at home when Felix gets out of surgery, to let you know how he's doing? I think you've had enough for one day, don't you?"

"If only you knew . . ." *you wouldn't be here being so sweet to me,* she thought, and it hurt so much, her mind limped back to limbo. It was easier and safer and a lot less painful to let him do all the thinking right now. "That's a good idea."

Though he'd had her heart for some time she relinquished the rest of herself, body and soul, into his keeping. He handled them with the same quiet, authoritative gentleness her heart had come to recognize as his innate nature—that which the too-nice person inside her, what was left of her anyway, had bonded with the first time she'd seen him.

He did it all. Introduced himself to the rest of her family, made arrangements with Bobby to have her car and the clutch wallet she'd left inside returned to her house, asked her mother to call when Felix was out of the woods, whisked her out of the hospital, and drove her home before she could think twice. When he reached for the spare key she kept hidden over the door, she came out of her daze enough to ask how he'd known about it.

He laughed, and, pointing to the trash bag on one side of the door and the bare floor on the other, he said, "No flower pot, no rock in the garden, no mat in front of the door. So unless you keep it under your trash, where else would you keep it?"

He really knew people. He'd studied them for so long, their actions and reactions—maybe that was why *not* knowing his father had left him with such an overwhelming passion to figure him out that it often superseded the resentment he felt. And why hadn't Eugene taken the trash down yet? These thoughts passed through her jumbled mind like roadside billboards and were immediately forgotten.

Once inside, he shooed her off to the bathroom, leaving her to choose between a soak in the tub or a good hot shower while he rifled through her medicine cabinet for the aspirin she kept in the kitchen.

Okay, so maybe he didn't know *her* very well. . . . He thought she was a confident, tough, not-so-nice woman who knew what she wanted from life and didn't have any qualms about reaching out and taking it. He thought she was impulsive and blunt. He liked her attitude. In fact, most of what he knew and liked about her was . . . experimental.

He passed two white tablets and a glass of water around the shower curtain, and a few minutes later, a towel when she turned the water off. He was gone when she pushed the plastic aside, but the terry robe and the long cotton T-shirt she left hanging on the bathroom door were looped over the towel rack within easy reach. When she and the steamy mist emerged from the bathroom, she found the bed she hadn't made that morning turned down, the sheets smoothed and straightened. Looking like a haven for the beaten and weary.

Jonah was waiting for her. And he *did* know people, her tired mind insisted. He just didn't know the real her.

"Feel better?" he asked, his smile hopeful. She nodded.

"I never make my bed," she said impulsively, feeling an urge to tell him one true thing about herself that wasn't part of the well-balanced woman she was pretending to be. "I never have time in the morning and by the time I get home at night I figure I'm going to be crawling back into it in a few hours anyway, so what's the point?"

"Exactly. You'd think someone would come up with a sleeping arrangement that did away with all the paraphernalia. The blankets and sheets and pillows . . ." his voice trailed off when she untied the robe and shrugged it off, but she didn't notice. She threw it over the foot of the bed and climbed in.

She didn't notice his smile either, or the blend of humor, sympathy, lust, and affection in his eyes. He'd seen battle-weary fighter pilots on the aircraft carriers he'd been assigned to with the same flat, dazed expression on their faces, from too much stress and too little sleep. It broke his heart to see her this way. There were bruises and scratches all over her arms and legs—and the rest of her torso, too, he wagered. And not one complaint had she uttered. She was a real trouper.

"Your mother called while you were in the shower,"

he said, watching her shake her damp red hair aside so she didn't have to lie with it against her face. She lay down on her left side, felt the lump on her head, and rolled over to her right side, facing him. "Felix is out of surgery and heading up to his room. She said he was groggy, but not in any pain. Sleeping mostly. She thinks you should do the same."

"That's good," she said, to both Felix's condition and her mother's recommendation. She closed her eyes, reached out for the darkness that was waiting to consume her. She felt his lips at her temple and opened them again. "You're not leaving, are you? Or maybe you should. I don't know. You decide. Jonah?" she said, an urgency to her voice as she tried to shake the apathy and fatigue from her brain. "We need to talk."

"Now?"

"No. I'm too . . . tired, right now. It wouldn't come out right." She closed her eyes again. There was an ache in her chest, around her heart, as she realized how good it felt to have him there with her, caring for her, caring about her. Her little apartment felt more like a home with him in it. A peaceful place. A perfect place—except for one thing . . . "But soon. There are things about me you should know."

"Just don't tell me you're a mercenary, okay?" he said, repeating words she'd once used on him as he tucked the sheets and thin summer blanket around her. "I'm not at all sure how I'll react to that." It almost hurt, but she chuckled anyway. "I'm going to stay awhile, until I know you're asleep. Does your cat stay in or go out at night?"

Too sleepy to explain about Bubba, she muttered, "Out," and started to drift off—except for the one part of her that held tight; that heard him clear out and settle into the chair across from the bed; that could picture him watching over her like a guardian angel. That part of her that couldn't drift—wouldn't rest until she murmured, "Thank you, Jonah."

CHAPTER NINE

STEP NINE

Act the part and you will become the part.
—William James

*They say you are what you eat. But that doesn't mean
that if you eat a banana you become a banana. Fortu-
nately, or unfortunately, the same cannot be said of
who you are and how you act, because more often than
not, how you act is who you appear to be. So show the
world who you are.*

Ellen woke to the sight of a single yellow rosebud
on the pillow beside her, its sweet scent in the air
around her. Her lips slipped into a lazy smile as she
realized Jonah had snitched it from Mrs. Phipps's garden for her. She knew he was gone even before her gaze
focused on the chair he'd settled in the night before—it
was that quiet and empty in her little apartment. She
sighed. Her little apartment had never felt empty to her
before. Come to think of it, *she* felt empty too. She

pulled the covers tight about her, pulling all her energy inward, trying to fill the hollowness inside her.

It didn't work. She huffed out a frustrated breath and rolled onto her back. She stretched muscles that felt as if they'd been run over by a train, and sought a positive perspective. The sun was up and it was another bright, glorious summer day, she told herself, throwing the covers off, then scrambling to retrieve them before they lost all their heat to the chill of the air. Okay, so the sun was barely up, she noted with a glance at her alarm clock, and thinking positive wasn't going to make it any warmer. She quickly abdicated to the truth. She was going to feel hollow *and* cold until she was truthful with Jonah.

She tiptoed hurriedly to the bathroom, grabbing her robe and slippers on the way, and ten minutes later she had the phone tucked between her shoulder and chin while she made coffee, checking on Felix. He'd spent a quiet night and was doing fine, the nurse told her. She left a message that she'd be in to see him around noon—simultaneously deciding that she'd go to work that day in spite of bruises and aching muscles. After all, the whole world didn't need to know what an idiot she was, or how dangerously close she'd come to getting her brother killed, did it?

She'd go to work and *act* as if nothing were out of the ordinary and maybe it would *appear* that way.

Rising early proved to be convenient when one felt like the kink in the middle of a pretzel. Another long shower limbered her up a little. And a long skirt with a long-sleeved blouse, cuffs rolled up to the elbows, did much to hide all the scrapes and bruises. And though she wasn't quite feeling it, she did think she *looked* halfway human when she left her apartment—and found the trash bag Eugene *still* hadn't taken to the dumpster. Casting a perturbed glance at her neighbor's door, she decided to leave it until after work, not at all sure she'd be able to tote her trash and maneuver the stairs at the same time.

It was slow going, but she made it to her car. She'd found her keys and wallet on the coffee table and her car parked out in front of the house, instead of the rear. Getting into it was an exercise in pain management that she didn't look forward to repeating when it came time to get out again.

As it happened, however, she had enough pride left in her to walk into the bank standing tall, and if she sat down at her desk a bit gingerly, no one seemed to notice. She turned on her computer, put her purse in the bottom drawer of her desk, removed a fresh notepad from her top drawer, smiled at Joleen Powers and Mary Westford when they came through the door, and then she frowned.

Something was wrong. She could feel it as surely as she felt the pain in her left hip and shoulder and the nagging stiffness in her neck. Something was very wrong. She could see it in their faces, sense it in the polite smiles they returned—smiles that held none of the friendship and fondness she'd come to expect from both of them.

Perhaps the paranoia she'd felt the day before wasn't just in her head. Maybe she'd been so distracted lately, she'd inadvertently offended one of them. Maybe she'd made a mistake or an error. No, they would have said something about it, if it were that simple. Maybe she'd forgotten someone's birthday? No, no birthdays until next month, she noted on her calendar.

When Vi arrived moments later and gave her the same insincere smile, her heart sank to her feet.

"Hi," she said.

"Morning," Vi replied, going directly into her own cubicle without stopping at Ellen's.

"Did you do anything fun last night?"

"Nope." No in-depth report of her latest conquest? No jolly anecdotes about the women on her bowling team? No gossip? No new fashion tips or self-improvement advice?

Ellen tapped her thumbs together nervously. "Anything new with you?"

"Nope." There was *always* something new with her.

"Have you heard—"

"I've got work to do, okay?"

"Sure. Okay."

One by one, she received the same cool, polite treatment from the rest of the bank's employees, except for Lisa Lee. Her smile was as warm and broad as ever, and Ellen was grateful for it. She went back for seconds and thirds, as a matter of fact, she was so desperate for the friendly camaraderie she was used to receiving from her fellow workers. Especially when she hurt and felt so much guilt for what she'd done to Felix—and for what she hadn't told Jonah.

Jonah . . . For the hundredth time she looked over at the camera shop to see the Closed sign dangling on the door and wondered where he was. Visiting his father was her most likely answer, but he rarely stayed so long. And he hadn't called her to see how she was, or Felix was, or to report that his father wasn't doing well.

She waited till ten before she called to check on both Felix and Earl Blake, who were both stable, the nurses told her. She asked if Jonah was visiting with his father, only to be told he'd been in earlier and left already. So where was he?

And all the while the furtive glances and chilly demeanor of those around her ate away at her dwindling confidence and sense of well-being, so that when Vi left the window a little before noon to use the ladies' room, she gathered up what she had left of her courage and followed her.

Vi was washing her hands when Ellen entered. Vi gave her a quick look in the mirror and muttered, "It's all yours. I'll be out in a second."

"I don't want it. I want you to tell me what's going on around here. I want you to tell me why you're acting so weird." She threw up both hands. "Why everyone's acting so weird."

"We're acting weird?" Vi grabbed a paper towel from the dispenser and wadded it in her hands. "What about you? You're the only one who's acting weird around here." She tossed the paper into the trash. "And if this is what dating a hunky camera salesmen does to you, well, let's just say it isn't pretty."

"Is that what this is about? You're angry because I'm dating Jonah? Because you wanted him? I didn't—"

Vi laughed a mirthless laugh. "I don't care who you date. You can have Jonah, if you want him. There are plenty of other men. But if you're only dating him because you thought I wanted him, then you're worse off than I thought."

"I'm not . . . I didn't . . . I . . . I love him. I didn't think it would matter to you."

"It doesn't," she said, almost hissing the words. "You could have told me you were going after him, but it doesn't really matter and it doesn't have anything to do with this other business."

"What other business?" she asked, both hands out in supplication. "What else have I done?"

"Leaving early, taking long lunches on busy days."

"Oh. You've never taken a long lunch?"

"Not on a crazy-busy day," she said, and seeming to realize this point might be debatable, she hurried on to the next. "And you knew Lisa was saving money to bring her mother over here from Korea. You knew she wanted Mary's job in Loans for the extra money so she could bring her over sooner. And you marched right into Joleen's office and snatched that job right out from under her. And what for? It's only temporary. You don't get brownie points for knowing all that stuff. You *know* you won't be able to give loans to everyone who wants one—and the old Ellen we all knew and loved would have hated having to turn someone down. So why'd you do it? Just to be mean? Is it because she's Korean?"

"No. No. I . . . No."

"You know what's really sad about all this? She thought filling in for Mary was an honor. An honor for you because you'd trained her and an honor for her to be able to help out Mary. She's perfectly willing for you to have *all* the honor of helping our friend Mary, and she refuses to admit she's disappointed that her mother won't be coming sooner. But she was so excited before. Really, Ellen, it was a lousy thing to do."

"I . . . I didn't know. I mean, I did know . . . that she was saving to bring her mother over. But I didn't know that's why she wanted the job. I didn't think . . . It never occurred to me. I . . . Oh, God. What have I done?"

Vi studied her for a second or two, then backed off even as she took a step forward.

"You really didn't know, did you?" Ellen shook her

head and Vi looked a bit sheepish. "Maybe I should have guessed that when Sylvia said that Joleen said you were adamant about having the job. Adamant just doesn't sound like you."

"No. I was adamant. I found out Lisa was making fifty cents an hour more than I was and that they were thinking of letting her fill in for Mary . . . and they hadn't even asked me to and . . . well, I was adamant. Very adamant. I didn't think about Lisa, didn't even give Joleen time to explain the situation to me. I . . . I didn't even want the job. It was the principle of it all. I was standing up for myself, not trying to hurt Lisa."

She felt horrible, could hardly look Vi in the eye. If she'd known all the facts, she wouldn't have done it. The last thing she wanted to do was to delay the reunion of Lisa and her mother.

"That's probably what threw us all off in the first place," Vi said, breaking the fragile silence between them. And when Ellen looked up in confusion, she added, "You standing up for yourself." Then she grinned. "Very out of character, but not a bad thing. Maybe you should have given us a warning or something. Put us on alert." Ellen chuckled a little and Vi laughed out loud and looped an arm around her shoulder. "Maybe this camera guy, Jonah, is having a positive influence on you. You better tell me all about it. Start with the sex." They were leaving the restroom when she came up short. "But first tell me how much you make an hour. If Lisa's making more than me, too, I'm going to want you to have another little talk with Joleen."

Ellen laughed and then sucked in air when their hips bumped passing through the doorway.

"What? What happened? What's wrong?" Vi asked,

her face a mask of concern at the pain in her friend's face.

Ellen sighed and, needing a friend, told Vi the whole story in as few words as possible as they walked slowly back to their cubicles in the window. However, she carefully forgot to mention where she'd gotten her inspiration for her escapades that week.

"Jeez," Vi said at the end of the tale, leaning against the petition between their desks. "No wonder you've been acting so weird. Underpaid. Beaten up. *And* no sex?"

"I knew you'd put it all in perspective for me." She leaned back in her chair, feeling totally drained.

"You know, you shouldn't be here today," Vi said. Ellen looked up and raised her brows to remind Vi of their conversation in the restroom. "No. I mean it. It's been pretty slow today; I can handle it alone. Let me get some lunch, then you go check on Felix and go home, take care of yourself. That's your biggest problem, you know. You take better care of everyone else than you do yourself."

It seemed to Ellen those were the very words that had gotten her into this mess to begin with, but she was too tired to argue.

While Vi was at lunch, she had another, much shorter meeting with Joleen—who was so delighted to be able to make harmony reign among her employees again, she didn't hesitate to give her the rest of the afternoon off.

The nurses related that Felix had been medicated for pain and might be sleeping, and that she'd missed her mother and sister by a good fifteen minutes. It was just as well. Truth be told, she wasn't eager to face any of them in broad daylight. Given the time to think, now that the crisis was over, she was fairly certain they wouldn't be looking at her kindly. Not after the part she'd played in getting Felix beaten to a pulp.

She stepped silently into his room, stood there for several minutes to make sure he was sleeping, then crept closer to the bed. His left eye was hideously swollen and blue-black, along with several other places on his once handsome face. His cheeks were puffed out, as if he had a walnut stuffed in each one, and he was breathing through his mouth. She could see a mishmash of wires across his teeth, locking his jaws together. His right arm was bent at the elbow and encased in a large plaster cast, elevated on a pillow and taped to the bed rail, so the fingers were in the air, curled loosely over the end of the cast. She touched them gently with her index finger, feeling their warmth, noting they were slightly swollen as well.

She stood there for a long time listening to him breathe, in and out, and felt the whole situation take on a certain unrealness—as if it were all a bad dream and she'd be waking up soon. After all, how could she ever possibly have believed she could solve his problems all by herself? Oh, it was one thing to think she could solve her own problems—and hadn't *that* turned out well?— but to presume she could wave her little green book around and magically solve Felix's troubles as well was . . . unreal. She'd been dreaming.

No. She'd been a fool.

Tears clouded her vision. She really wanted to have a good cry, but she didn't want Felix to wake up and find her blubbering over his bed, so she turned and left the room, taking the first exit she saw. But instead of leaving the building or going down to the basement to the cafeteria, she took the ascending stairs and wound up on the second floor, a few doors down from Earl Blake's room.

She didn't really want Jonah to see her crying either, but if she could get him to hold her for a minute or two . . . Oh, the thought of it filled her with such yearning, it seemed to hollow her out like a cored apple, she needed him so much. If she could get him to hold her for a minute or two, she knew this overwhelming feeling of being hopelessly stupid and incompetent and so totally, totally wrong about everything in her life would stop spreading, would maybe ease a little, or even go away. Because aside from the fact that she'd pretended to be someone she wasn't in the beginning, what she'd come to feel for Jonah was the one true, unshakable, absolutely right thing she'd done all week—maybe in her whole life.

Blinking her eyes clear, she approached Earl's room with great hope of finding Jonah inside. But he wasn't. Earl lay in his bed, his lifeless eyes wide open, his body angled to the right a bit, the sheets folded back and tucked in tight.

"Aw, Earl," she said, sighing as she entered the room and walked toward the man in the bed. "We blew it big time, didn't we?" She studied his wrinkled face, and even the lines that were supposed to give his face character and tell a thousand stories about his life didn't reveal a single element of his personality. "You know, if there really was some sort of magic potion I could use to change another person's life, I'd use it on you. And you'd be glad I did. You would," she said, tugging on the tight sheet, loosening it so it draped in a more natural fashion. "You missed something really wonderful in your life." She hesitated. "It sure doesn't take very long to screw things up, does it? Took me about a week. How long did it take you to decide that Jonah would be better off at a boarding school than wandering all over the world with an eccentric, self-absorbed loner like you? Ten minutes? A month?" She paused. "Strange, isn't it, the way some mistakes can be fixed, and some— no matter how much you want it—can't be undone." She sighed again. "You probably already know this, but I'm going to tell you anyway. Your son, Jonah, is a good man. He's kind and sweet and smart, really smart. And he's got *so* much love to give . . . maybe because you weren't around to give it to or maybe it's just the way he is. I don't know. And I don't know if he'll ever set the world on fire, or if he even wants to, but you should be really proud of him. I love him, Mr. Blake. And I'm going to keep on loving him, as hard as I can, for as long as I can." She gave him one last chance to respond, but he didn't. "I just thought you'd like to know all that."

She gave his thin, bony shoulder a friendly, reassuring pat and left the room.

She hadn't realized how truly bone weary she was until she pulled into her parking space behind the lovely old Victorian house and took the key from the ignition. She leaned back in the seat and closed her eyes. The weight of the world pressed heavily on her chest. Her life was a mess. All she wanted to do was curl up in Jonah's arms and let him take care of her, just for a little while, until her muscles stopped aching and her energy returned. Then she'd fix everything, she'd make her life right again, turn it all around. She would.

She opened her eyes and opened the car door. Of course, the next best thing to having Jonah baby her a little would be some tea and sympathy from Mrs. Phipps. She'd fuss over her and do all the talking. Ellen could sit there and sip warm Earl Grey; listen to Bubba purr and not think.

Coming home early, she hadn't expected to see Mrs. Phipps on the back porch waiting for her, but she was disappointed anyway. She needed a friend, and in a perfect world friends would be there, waiting.

She wasn't sure what drew her gaze to the rearview mirror, but she did a double take, then turned her head to see the object of her wishful thinking walking briskly across the drive behind her car with a small wire push-cart in tow.

"Mrs. Phipps," she said, getting out of the car as quickly as her battered body allowed. "I was just thinking about you." She stopped and turned toward her, a bright smile as her greeting. "How are you feeling?"

"Just fine, dear. And how are you? We've missed you this week."

"I've missed you too," she said, walking up to her. Motioning to the small bag of groceries in the pushcart, she asked, "Can I help you with that?"

"No, no. It's nothing, dear. We can manage it."

"It's pretty hot out this afternoon. Should you be out walking in this heat?"

"Well, my goodness, why not?" She laughed cheerfully. "When we were young, we walked all the time. Heat. Snow. Rain. When my son was little, he used to *run* the three blocks to the grocery. Of course, he always had that extra dime I'd give him for candy, burning a hole in his pocket." She chuckled at the memory.

They reached the back door and Ellen held it open for her, lifting the back of the pushcart off the ground to help her over the threshold.

"Felix is in the hospital," she said. "I—"

"My, my, my." She shook her head. "I know. I know. How is he? Have you been to see him? Your young man was here this morning and *he* told me the news."

"Jonah? Jonah was here this morning?"

"Yes, dear. A little after nine. We stepped out to tell him that he'd just missed you." She chuckled. "He had two little cups of coffee and a bag of store-bought muffins. He offered to share his coffee with us, since you were already gone but, of course, we don't drink coffee, so he came in while we made tea and we sat and had a nice little visit." She shook her head again, remembering. "Felix. How is he doing, dear? Your young man hadn't been to the hospital yet; he didn't know much."

"He's fine, I guess, considering." She didn't really want to think about this right now. She wanted tea. She wanted pity. "I just left him. His mouth is wired closed and his arm is in a cast and he has bruises all over, but the nurses say he's fine."

"So sad. Such a dear, sweet boy, when he's not under the weather."

They were walking down the hall, toward her door. Ellen could almost taste the tea already.

"He wasn't under the weather when this happened, you know, he—"

"Well, we won't keep you, dear," she said when they reached her door. "Your young man said you weren't feeling well and you do look tired." She hesitated. "Do you need anything?"

"Well . . ." She'd been hoping for the familiar invitation to tea, but it didn't look as if it was coming. Good thing she wasn't too nice anymore. "I was hoping we could have tea."

Mrs. Phipps's head tipped to one side as she considered her neighbor with great fondness.

"You are such a dear, sweet girl, Ellen," she said, her voice cracking with feeling. She stepped forward and put a hand on Ellen's arm. "But you don't have to have tea with us anymore, dear. In fact, I think we owe you an apology." Ellen would have stopped her if she knew what she was talking about. Instead she stood in stunned silence while Mrs. Phipps said, "The past few days have made us realize that we've been abusing your friendship, and we never meant to do that. We . . . we get lonely sometimes, and we so very much enjoy your company that . . ." She lowered her voice to a whisper. "Well, we'd think up things for you to buy at the store so you'd have to stop by every evening and chat with us." The sincerity in her expression was tearing Ellen to shreds. Her throat was tight and tears were pushing at her eyes. She was afraid to speak for fear the wail of despair building inside her would cut loose and bring the house down on both of them. "We didn't stop to think that you were young and busy and had better things to do with your time than sit around having tea with an old woman and her cat. Goodness, we were young once. We remember how it is."

Ellen wanted to die. Just lie down on the floor and die. Nothing, not one thing she'd done that week, had been anything but a well-intentioned attempt to improve her own life, and yet she'd done nothing but hurt other people in the process.

"But we're mending our ways," Mrs. Phipps said. "We'll be doing our own shopping from now on, and we won't press you to have tea with us so often. Any time you feel like coming down, we'll be delighted to see you. We love you, dear. Come when you have the time to spare and only when you really want to."

It crossed Ellen's mind to fall on her knees and beg the old lady's forgiveness, but she had a feeling that she'd never get up again if she did. How had she managed to hurt the kindest woman in the world?

"This week has been a little unusual," she said, feeling as flat and heavy as an anvil. "And maybe I am a little tired," she added, starting up the stairs to her apartment. "But Mrs. Phipps?" She look over the banister at her. "I love having tea with you."

The woman smiled and nodded. "Then you come down when you've rested up a bit and we'll have some."

She smiled back at her, hoping everything she'd screwed up that week was as easy to fix; that everyone she'd hurt or deceived was as forgiving and understanding. Then she saw the trash bag still propped against the wall outside her door. She trudged to the top step and stood staring at it, then over at Eugene's door. Apparently even small rodentlike people who lived in the dark were not without feelings. No food, no neighborly trash disposal. She looked back at the small white plastic bag of trash.

She'd have to think this one over.

She let herself into the apartment, closed the door, and leaned back against it. Her eyes closed automatically—in relief, but in self-defense too. Her mind was too numb to take in one more thought, one more ounce of guilt or even half a question. All she wanted to do was sleep, close out the world, hide for a little while.

She opened her eyes and the first thing she saw was not the blinking light on her answering machine telling her she had nine messages waiting, but the purse she'd used two nights ago, tossed upside down in the chair.

The purse with the teal blue negligee wrapped so carefully in tissue, hope and excitement inside. Jonah wedged his way back into her thoughts, pushed everything else aside, putting more pressure on her heart than she ever dreamed possible. Part of her desperately wanted him there, to hold her and comfort her. Another part wanted him there so she could finally be honest with him. But another part was dreading their next encounter, afraid of the truth, afraid of disappointing him, afraid that being herself wouldn't be enough for him.

She picked up the purse and kicked off her shoes on her way to the bedroom, and that was all she could remember. She was asleep in seconds.

CHAPTER TEN

STEP TEN

It requires wisdom to understand wisdom;
the music is nothing if the audience is deaf.
    —*Walter Lippmann*

Don't beat your head against walls. It's not only stupid,
it's disfiguring. Any gambler will tell you that you
have to know when to hold and when to fold. Choose
your battles carefully. And remember, failure isn't
really failure if a lesson's been learned.

Okay, so some people had to be hit with baseball
bats. It wasn't going to take more than one good whack
on the head for Ellen to figure things out. And okay, so
she'd bought a pamphlet from the grocery store and
followed the advice in it. That didn't *really* make her a
fool. So okay! Where did she go from there? How did
she go about reclaiming her peace of mind?

She came awake at dusk feeling a little stronger but
no better. She felt restless and disjointed. She sat on the

edge of the bed for some time, her mind in a muddle, hating what she'd done to her life and yet easily recalling the frustrations of being too nice.

Frustration or guilt? They tipped the scale evenly, pushed and pulled with equal force, and there she was in the middle—miserable.

A shower made things cleaner but no clearer. She couldn't even decide what to wear. Get dressed? Get ready for bed? Take care of herself or take care of others? Go back to the hospital to be with Felix? Stay home? With the damp towel still wrapped tight about her, she plopped down on the edge of the bed and fell backward with her arms spread wide, her hand brushing the purse she'd stumbled into bed with earlier. Turning her head, she looked at it mindlessly for several minutes, then picked it up, holding it over her head as she unzipped it.

The teal blue silk spilled out like so much water from a glass and pooled on her bare chest, cool and soft. Untangling the tissue and tossing it aside, she held the gown up in front of her. So beautiful, and such a waste. She sighed. Some seductress she was. She wore T-shirts to bed, flannel in the winter—she was no seductress. She could barely manipulate sheets onto a bed, much less Jonah.

This was going to be another huge disappointment to him, she thought, sitting up and slipping the silk on over her head—standing and feeling it slither down the curves of her body like a lover's caress. She looked at herself in the mirror, turned from side to side, smiled. Then she laughed at the thought of having it dry-cleaned every time she wore it. It was beautiful, but it wasn't her. She wasn't some tightly wrapped, sophisticated, self-confident vamp who took what she wanted from the world. She was . . . Ellen.

Not a bad person. Not a hurtful person. Not a perfect person. Just Ellen—who liked seeing other people happy, who enjoyed feeling needed, who felt satisfied in knowing she could assert herself when she had to, who didn't—

She picked up her head and listened to what she thought was a cat crying somewhere. Bubba crying outside her door? He never did that, she thought, frowning as she, in her teal blue nightgown, went to the door barefoot. He was too lazy to cry when he wanted in or out—he usually just lay there sleeping until someone came along to accommodate him.

"What's the matter, baby, are you sick?" she asked him when she opened the door and found him sitting there in no obvious distress. She stooped down. "You hurt? Or just lonely?" He stared at her, making no attempt to scoot by her into the apartment. Another victim of her crusade for change? It was hard to tell with Bubba. "You fiddled around in the doorway too long and she closed it on you, didn't she?" She sighed, thinking of her own situation. If she fiddled around much longer, Jonah would never get to know the real Ellen. He'd be leaving town eventually, going back to his life. She didn't want that door to close on her. "Well, it happens sometimes. Want me to go down and get her to open it back up for you?" She wasn't above making amends to a cat. She frowned on a new thought: maybe he was acting strange because something had happened to Mrs. Phipps. "Let's go check on her."

They walked to the top of the stairs and saw Jonah at the bottom, his foot on the first step. He stood there looking up at her, the concern in his expression almost obliterated by the desire that sprang into his eyes. She felt feverish, going hot and then cold, chills running in waves across her skin. He was so handsome. So tall and strong and sweet and gentle. Her heart felt overly full, the pressure in her chest building until she thought it might rip her apart. She raised her hand to her breast to control it, felt warm skin and silk and suddenly recalled what she was wearing.

"I . . . I wasn't expecting to see you," she said, feeling self-conscious. Making a sincere confession in a seductive negligee seemed a little contradictory.

"You should have been," he said, moving up to the first step. "I've been trying to get you all day."

She took a step down, saying, "I forgot to look at my machine. I was tired."

He nodded, taking another step up, his eyes riveted. He could barely breath, she was so beautiful, her skin so pale against the gray-blue silk, her glorious red hair soft and curly, a little damp yet on the ends from her shower. He didn't know how he continued to speak. "I know. I finally called Mrs. Phipps to see if you'd shown up here. I was surprised you went to work today, and then worried when you went home early."

"I'm sorry. I should have called you," she said, taking another step toward him.

He shook his head and took another step. "It doesn't matter. As long as you're all right. *Are* you all right?"

She'd taken one more step down before she started to shake her head at him. "No. I'm not all right. I'm all wrong."

He took the rest of the steps two at a time until there was only one between them, and Bubba was sitting on it. On closer inspection Jonah could see that whatever was all wrong about her, it wasn't physical. There was a sadness in her eyes, but they were clear and bright; and though she was pale, her skin had a warm, healthy glow to it. He couldn't stop himself from reaching out and touching a flyaway curl near her cheek, nor did he pull his hand away when she inclined her head to meet his touch.

"You don't look all wrong," he said. "You look beautiful."

"Appearances can be deceiving," she said, unwilling to look at him, sure that she couldn't bear to watch whatever he found beautiful in her fade in his eyes. "And I've been deceiving you."

His heart stopped and his knees grew weak with foreboding. He felt his world slipping away from him and lowered himself to the step below hers. Deceiving him? Ellen? His heart sputtered and pumped a little blood to his head. That didn't make sense. His pulse took on a steadier rhythm. Though their relationship was less than a week old, he knew her. Knew her so well, his soul felt every breath she took as if it were his own. Knew her so well that for the first time in his life he hadn't needed to second-guess himself. Knew her so well, he'd invested every drop of his faith and trust in her. He knew her that well.

"Deceiving me how?" he asked, convinced now that this was more about her than him, and he was dying to hear it. He wanted her more than any woman he'd ever known. Body and soul. In good times and bad.

When she looked at him, her expression was so forlorn that had it been another time and place, he would have stood up and fought off dragons and dark knights with his sword for her—but as it was, he had to sit and wait for her to reveal what evil demons were after her.

"Some people . . ." she said, looking away briefly and then back at him, not knowing how to start. She was simply going have to say it. "I'm too nice." His brows lifted in surprised agreement, but before he could speak, she stopped him. "No, you don't understand. I'm too nice for my own good sometimes—at least I thought I was. Now I'm not so sure. No, I am. I know I am. So I tried to change. But being someone I'm not didn't work out very well either—except for my pay raise and this thing with Eugene—unless his feelings are hurt and to tell you the truth I'm not sure if I care about that either, which leads me to believe more of this person that I'm *not* has rubbed off on me and I'm not at all sure I want that because I've hurt just about every person I care about and . . ."

"Ellen. Ellen," he said hastily when she paused briefly to take in air. "Ellen. Maybe you should start at the beginning."

She frowned. The beginning? Where was that? Her birth? Early childhood? She'd been too nice for as long as she could remember. She sighed, then took in a deep breath and started over.

"I'm a nice person."

"I know you are."

"But not *just* a nice person. I'm too nice." She'd lost him again, she could tell. He'd reached out to finger her hair while she talked, looking at it as if it were spun gold. She took his hand in hers and held it in her lap. "I don't honk my horn and flip people off when they pull into a parking space I've been waiting five minutes for, and I don't scream or curse at people who don't stop to say thank you after I've helped them pick up the mountain of cracker boxes their kid knocked over. I didn't even get mad when I found out Lisa Lee was making

more money than me—hurt and disappointed, sure—
but not mad. Never mad and never . . ." She shook
her fist, looking for the right word. "Never . . .
what?"

"Irate?"

"No."

"Outraged?"

"No. Not really."

"Then I don't know."

"I don't either," she said, giving him a small smile.
"What is it that those people have that makes them
speak up when someone cuts in line in front of them? I
would assume they were in more of a hurry than I was,
or had an emergency, or left their kids in the car, or
something—not that they were just being rude for the
heck of it or that they should be at the end of the line
no matter what. You see how I am? See how my mind
works?"

He could tell she was serious about this. "But I like
the way your mind works."

"Well, I don't," she said, leaning back, away from
him. She didn't want his approval. She wanted him to
understand. "I'm sick of letting old men go ahead of me
in line and watching them win the Anniversary Jackpot.
And I'm sick of letting my brother use my apartment
like a flophouse every time he gets too drunk to find his
way home. I'm sick of people stealing my vacation spots
and my parking spaces and my leftover food. And I'm
sick of standing aside when someone else shows an interest in a man I'm interested in or a job I want or . . .
or anything else I want—"

"Whoa, whoa, whoa. Back up a second. What about
this man you're interested in?" Now he was leaning
back, away from her and very confused. She'd said they

needed to talk but . . . No, he couldn't have been that
wrong about her. He just couldn't have been.

"That's what started all this," she said. She hadn't
meant to get into this can of worms, but now that it was
open, why not tip it over and dump everything out?
"Well, it wasn't the only thing, it was like the fuse on
the end of a stick of dynamite. You smiled at Vi from
across the street and for just a few seconds I thought
you were smiling at me and . . ." She glared at him. "I
wanted you to smile at *me*, Jonah. I wanted you to see
me. But I knew that would never happen once you met
Vi, because she's so— What? Why are you laughing?"

"Because I did see you. I—"

"No, don't. Don't try to make me feel better. Just
listen to me. Stop that," she said when he sat there
grinning at her. "I'm serious about this, but if you don't
want to hear what I have to say . . ."

"No. Sit. Please. I'm sorry. Go on," he said, bowing
his head so she couldn't see the joy in his eyes, laboring
to control his smile. "I want to hear it all."

Mildly miffed that he was having such a good time
at her expense, she slowly started again. "I understand
why men are attracted to bold, self-confident women
like Vi. I do. And I don't blame them. I like Vi. I like
the way she goes after what she wants. I like that she's
not afraid to try new things and say what she thinks and
do whatever crosses her mind. I'd be like that if I knew
how. I just didn't know how—until I found the little
green book."

"The little green book?"

"Well, it's not even a book really," she said, and
quickly explained how and where and why she'd gotten
her primer for personal growth. "You're not laughing
again, are you?"

"No." He said it emphatically to convince them both. "I'm not laughing."

"And I'm not saying it's a Bible or anything like that," she said defensively. "Sometimes it isn't possible to scratch where it itches at the exact time you're itching."

"What?"

"Never mind," she said, feeling a rush of heat in her cheeks. "Some of the steps in that little book were great. Like attitude, I love having an attitude, it's like pretending you're somebody else—except it's hard to use on old ladies or cats. And thinking positive and saying no. Nothing else, just no. And being blunt with people, saying exactly what's on your mind, even in a nice way. It made me feel so powerful. In control. Even turning left and going that way, which is really just doing the exact opposite of what you'd normally do—that was exciting."

"Then what's the problem? It doesn't matter where you learned these things, as long as you learned them. There's nothing wrong with being assertive and self-confident."

She shook her head and looked down at her hands again. "That's not what I learned though. That's what I thought I was learning, what I wanted to learn, but . . . I wasn't using each step to improve myself. I was using them against other people. People I like. People I love, who are not always convenient to love." She looked up to see if he knew what she meant by that. His fathomless green eyes were soft with understanding. "I went from being too nice to being not too nice at all. Look what I did to Felix."

"What happened to Felix wasn't your fault," he said firmly.

"No. Not all of it. But my part of it was done, not out of love for my brother, but very selfishly to eliminate his problems as quickly as possible because he was being a problem to me. I used positive thinking and a whole lot of attitude to bully him into Krane's hands. Felix tried to tell me how dangerous he was, but I wouldn't believe him."

"Ellen, that whole situation was a mistake made by everyone involved. And your part in it may just be the only good thing to come of it."

"In what way? My brother looks like a truck backed over him. What good can come of that?"

"Well, for one thing, Officer Ingles said Felix nearly went insane when he heard you'd been within a hundred yards of Krane. You forced him to do the right thing by calling in the cops to protect you."

"To protect me?"

"Your testimony in court would be something Krane would never allow, especially if Felix happened to die as a result of his beating."

"You mean, he . . . I . . ."

He nodded. "He would have had to kill you too."

"And my mom and my sister?" She covered her face with her hands. She hadn't once considered this aspect of what she'd done, and the enormity of it was too horrible to envision.

He gently pried her hands away, holding them in his as he said, "That's not going to happen. It was never going to happen. Felix wouldn't let it happen. He did the right thing. And now he's in a safe place, drying out. This could be the best thing that ever happened to him."

"Or the worst."

"I don't think so," he said, and he was probably

right, she conceded. If what happened with Krane wasn't enough to set Felix on the path of the sober and righteous, then he was heading for something much, much worse. When she remained silent, contemplating what might have been, he finally tucked a finger under her chin to raise her eyes to his. They were thoughtful and wise and caring. "You made a mistake, Ellen. We all make mistakes."

She gave a slight nod. "I know. I just don't think I've ever made quite so many in one week before. It's . . . overwhelming," she said with a small smile. "Even little Mrs. Phipps. I told her no, over and over again. And not because I didn't want to have tea with her, but because I was using all my lunch hours shopping for her. And she was just lonely, just using the groceries as an excuse to get me to come have tea with her. I should have guessed. I should have told her it wasn't necessary and just had tea with her most afternoons, maybe shopped for her once a week or something. We could have worked things out if I hadn't acted so selfishly."

"Mrs. Phipps loves you. She'll understand. She'll forgive you. It was just another mistake and you've learned from it, so it wasn't really a mistake." She looked at him and he grinned. "It was a learning experience."

"Oh," she said, smiling, wishing she really could see more of the humor in it. He was right though, about making mistakes and learning from them. Being brave and daring enough to take what she wanted from the world was new to her; she was bound to make a few mistakes at first. Even the little green book advised aiming straight and choosing battles carefully. Maybe she just needed more practice. "And what about the mistake I made with you?"

"Meeting me wasn't a mistake," he said, beaming at her.

"No, but pretending to be something I wasn't was. Pretending to be bolder and more self-confident than I was, so you wouldn't know how nervous I was or how excited I was to be with you." She looked down at the teal blue silk draped gracefully over her legs. "Carrying this thing around in my purse, planning to seduce you the first chance I got. That was . . ."

"You had this in your purse?"

She nodded, shamefaced. "I just wanted to prove to myself that I could have someone like you in my life. I wanted you to think I was as sophisticated and capable as the other women you've known. That I wasn't just some too-nice person who had a quiet little job in a quiet little bank in a quiet little town that you could forget the second you were back in Washington."

"You had this in your purse?" he asked, his mind stuck on the idea.

"Yes."

"You were planning to seduce me?"

"Yes." The look on his face made her smile and released a thousand tiny butterflies in her stomach. "We had dinner with Felix instead."

He groaned and made a face that caused her to chuckle while he reached out to rub the silk between his fingers, his knuckles grazing the warm, soft skin above her sternum. Her heart started beating so fast, she thought she heard it whirring.

"I love this color," he said.

"I know."

His gaze met hers, held it in an unbreakable bond

that would link his soul to hers for all time. Despite the turmoil in her heart at present, below it lay the rock-solid base of love and kindness she was born with, and the peace and acceptance he'd yearned for all his life. There was no way for her to hide it, or change it, or destroy it. It would temper every step she took in life and reshape the world as he knew it.

"It's beautiful on you," he said, brushing the ends of her hair back over her shoulder, skimming the skin there as he went. "It would be a real shame to waste it." He leaned forward and dropped sweet soft kisses down the curve of her neck and shoulder.

Little shivers raced across her skin. "But what about the way I misled you?" Her arms felt rubbery as she pushed at him. "What about the real me and the way I pretended to be somebody I wasn't? What if you don't like the real me?"

"Well, first off," he said, brushing the thin strap from her shoulder—which she promptly replaced as he spoke—"I know the real you. I love the real you. And secondly"—he brushed the strap away again—"unless you've told me a flat out lie about yourself somewhere along the way, you haven't deceived me or misled me, you were just embellishing."

"Embellishing?" She wasn't really asking a question, just repeating the word. He was tracing the heart-shaped contour of the gown as it crossed her breasts, and the nerve endings in her brain were shooting sparks and shorting out one by one. How could she ask questions?

"Mmm, embellishing," he said, his finger in the valley between her breasts. They both watched as it began a slow ascent over the next slope. "Decorating the truth a little. People do it all the time to bolster their courage when they need a little extra. Like for job interviews or for meeting new people. Is this a mole or a freckle?"

"Um . . . a freckle." It could have been a tarantula for all she knew; her head was swimming with sensation and excitement as his fingers slid lightly over her shoulder and down her arm.

"I like it," he said, pressing his lips gently to hers. Soft and sweet. He kissed the corner of her mouth, then one side of her chin, her lower lip, the little dip below it, watching as her eyes closed. His hand snaked under the gown and found her ankle. "Now me," he said, slowly sprinkling kisses and moving his hand up her leg. "I prefer the ambush approach."

"Ambush," she muttered mindlessly.

"That's right. When I want to meet someone, I watch them through the bank window for about a month. Watch the way they interact with other people. Watch the way they sit and stand and hold their head when they're on the phone." Her eyes opened slowly to meet his. "I notice how kind they are to people. How nice they are when they don't have to be and . . . I fall in love with them."

"You do?" Her hand stopped his on her knee.

"Yes. I spend some time thinking maybe they're too nice for someone like me, that they might not like me, but my love is so strong, I decide it's worth the risk. Then I have a really hard time getting their attention. I wash the shop windows till they're paper thin, hoping they'll notice me. I hang out in the parking lot, hoping they'll see me and smile, so I can run up and introduce myself. I smile when I think they're looking my way, but they don't see me—or they pretend not to. Then one day I get lucky. Flimsy grocery bags."

"You did all that? You were watching me? Smiling at me?"

"For weeks."

She started to laugh, looping her arms about his neck, pulling him near, closing the small distance between them. Their lips met in joy that turned swiftly to passion, their hands grasping, skin warming as blood turned to fire in their veins. He pressed her back against the railing with just his lips, supporting his weight on one arm while the hand of the other slid up her thigh like a cool summer breeze . . . in fact, she *felt* a cool summer breeze.

"Jonah," she said, turning her head from side to side, trying to evade his mouth and clear her mind at the same time. "We can't do this here." She started to laugh, and he kissed her again.

"I'll give you a two-second start," he said, wrenching his mouth from hers as he pushed himself away.

Her head was spinning. "Two?"

"One."

Gathering silk in one hand, she used the other for support as she turned and scrambled up the stairs. He caught her half a second after she crossed into her apartment. His mouth was glued to hers before she heard the door close.

She could feel his feet shuffling out of his shoes while his hands raced from her gown to the front of his shirt and back again as he feverishly tried to get them both naked immediately. Breathless with excitement and lack of air, she fumbled with his belt buckle.

"I have a bed if you're interested," she said, laughing.

"I'm not," he said, pushing his pants to the floor and two-stepping out of them; reaching for her, pulling her near, palming and pressing her breast, his mouth everywhere he could find skin. The aching need in her swollen breasts turned to pure pleasure, dripping and oozing over her conscious mind like sweet, warm syrup. Her thoughts bunched together, grew thick and sticky and unintelligible.

"But . . . but what about my seduction?" she asked, feeling silk slide low on her breast and then off, gathering about her waist—his mouth exploring her inch by inch.

"It's perfect. It's great. I'm lost. Captivated. God, you taste good."

She giggled, then inhaled sharply at the sudden jolt of bliss as he clamped down on her nipple. "But . . . ah . . . this isn't . . . it."

It was several seconds before he raised his head to look at her. "It's not?" he asked, his voice raspy and strained. "Want me to stop?" She shook her head. "Okay, um . . ." He glanced down at her bare breasts, swallowed hard, closed his eyes, tried to think. "Oh, I know," he said, reaching for the teal blue gown—and since it wouldn't go any lower, began to raise it up over her head. "We'll take this off and save it for another time. I'll seduce you."

She gave a soft laugh and cooperated with his endeavor, but long before she stood naked before him they both knew there would be no leading the other astray, no matter whose seduction it was. It was what they both wanted, what their hearts yearned to reach out and take, and give in return. In a sort of unreal moment when even the air around them seemed charged with some magical force that made their coming together seem as inevitable and right as the earth's orbit around the sun, she placed her open palm on his chest, above his heart, to make sure she wasn't dreaming. Smooth, hard muscles strained against warm, soft skin; his heart hammered against her hand. . . .

His heart in her hand. It struck her as more than a metaphor as she met his gaze. The desire in his eyes matched her own. So did the love and the joy. But the fear that cast its shadow over his happiness was what her heart responded to most.

She smiled at him, sure for the first time that she possessed something no other woman could give him. Her hand moved up his chest, curved around the back of his neck, and she kissed him, felt his hands sliding up her body as he cleaved to her in a passionate embrace. She would take the heart he offered her, hold it gently in her hands. She would protect it, soothe it, fill it with joy and laughter, teach it to trust. With all she was, she tried to tell him that his heart was safe with her.

And maybe he understood. He wrenched his mouth suddenly from hers, his hand fisted in her hair, his breath coming hard and fast as he searched her face one last time in avid desperation for something he wasn't even sure he'd recognize. But he did. He saw it. The love, the acceptance, the faith she had in him.

He laughed out loud as he bent to scoop her up in his arms. She scattered kisses over his face as he carried her to the bed. He was aware of something busting loose inside him, bubbling and overflowing into every cell of his body. Rapture in its purest form, an unknown to him, and yet he recognized it instantly as something he needed in order to live—not just exist or survive on air and food and water as he had until that moment, but to truly live, with meaning and purpose.

He laid her gently on the bed, looming over her briefly with a smile—a special, significant smile meant just for her—before he lowered his mouth to hers and kissed her silly.

Earl Blake passed away that night. Silently and, Ellen would always attest, in peace. For she believed that despite his seemingly unconscious state, some part of Earl Blake had maintained residence inside that frail old body until the very last second, long enough for him to hear from her that his son would be well loved and cared for.

Of course, Jonah was never too sure of this theory, never really *sure* about anything pertaining to his father. He left Quincey with almost as many questions as he'd arrived with about the man, and yet somehow his death and funeral were like a seal of closure for him. Along with his father's body that day, he buried all his bitterness and resentment and with them went all notions of being unlovable, unworthy, and unacceptable.

Naturally, Ellen helped with that too. She thought him completely lovable, absolutely worthy, and totally acceptable. So much so, she married him in the fall, just as soon as Felix presented an appearance acceptable for the wedding photographs—which she was lucky to have, it all happened so fast.

With his hardship leave officially over, Jonah had to return to Washington. Three and a half weeks later he returned to Quincey. And, heart-stoppingly handsome in his dress-white uniform, he married Ellen on a Friday, then carried her over the threshold of his apartment in Anacostia, Maryland, that Sunday afternoon. For the next two months, every chance he got, he rambled with her from pillar to post, reseeing Washington through her eager eyes, even braving the frigid cold to watch the lighting of the National Christmas Tree.

She breathed life into the musty old museums and historical monuments that he'd barely given a second glance; brightened and defined each gloomy overcast day so that at the end of each month he had a string of distinct, individual days that meant something, rather than a block of days that ran together in a blur, exactly alike and meaningless. She was so full of life, figuratively and literally, they'd recently—and most joyfully—discovered.

"Guess who that was on the phone just now?" he said, bumping his way into the spare bedroom-cum-office with a pile of packing boxes. It still amazed him how quickly he'd gotten used to having her around, puttering around his things, *in* his life.

"Who?" she asked, sitting on the floor, packing up the books she'd so recently unpacked and put on the shelf he'd cleared out for her. They'd found a house in Upper Marlboro with four and a half acres of land on which Jonah was eager "to grow many children." She smiled warmly just thinking about it. He said he knew exactly what kind of father he didn't want to be, and he was so impatient to begin.

"Felix. He's adding cell phones and pagers to his inventory." He stretched out on the bed to watch her. It was his all-time favorite thing to do, watching her. "He says diversifying is the key to making that shop work, and he's looking into computer software and maybe even a line of computers after that."

She chuckled. "That little shop isn't going to hold him for long. Next thing you know, he'll be knocking down walls, expanding into the next building, bringing in wholesale refrigerators and microwaves and making Fast Felix ads for television."

At least she hoped so. She was so proud of him—and he was so proud of his four-month AA chip that he carried it around in his pocket and showed it to everyone he knew, her mother had reported. Jonah asking him to take over the camera shop had been good for his ego too.

"Yep. I think that's part of the plan," he said, watching her toss a handful of papers and brochures into the trash can. "Starring Mrs. Phipps as his best customer."

"Oh, she'd love that." She dropped more stuff in the can.

Earl's little white house had reverted back to the Gunthers when he passed away. Denise offered to let Felix rent it from her, but with Ellen's apartment being vacated and Mrs. Phipps so willing to mother and pamper him, he'd moved right in.

"Absolutely," he said, bellying his way to the edge of the bed to look into the trash can, since she seemed to be tossing more than she was packing. "Now that she's fixing hot meals for him and Eugene, he says he really wants to rent out that last downstairs apartment so there can be an even number for dinner every night." He reached into the can and removed a small green and white mini-book.

"Man, I wish she'd cooked real meals when I was there," she said, reaching for more papers and books to sort through. "Though eating with Eugene every night might have dampened my appetite quite a bit. I don't know how Felix stands it."

"He says he's not so bad, once you get used to him. Doesn't talk much. Scurries back to his room the minute he's finished eating," he said, raising his head to give her a perplexed look. "You know, I can't believe you're throwing this away."

Glancing over her shoulder, she grimaced. "Oh. Give me that," she said, snatching at the little green book, missing when he pulled his hand away. "Put it back in the trash. That thing has caused me nothing but trouble. I thought I threw it away back in Quincey."

"You did. I rescued it then too."

"Why?"

"I don't know, a keepsake maybe. Besides, I like some of these," he said, rolling onto his back, reading from the book as he held it above him. " *'Fill what's empty. Empty what's full. Scratch where it itches.'* That could be taken a lot of different ways. One way coming pleasantly to mind."

"Like you need a book to bring that to mind," she said, getting to her feet and snatching at it again. He let the arm farthest from her fall to the bed with the book in hand. She'd have to climb over him to get it—which by the look on his face was exactly what he was hoping she'd do. "You think you're pretty clever, don't you?" He nodded and smirked, and she couldn't bring herself to prove him otherwise.

She walked across the bed on her knees, straddled his midsection, and sat none too gently. "Ugh," he said with a whoosh of air. She leaned forward, pinning his arms to the bed.

"I don't need that little book anymore. I have everything I want right here. You. Our baby. A home." She paused. "The most important step was the one they saved for last anyway, and I have it down pat."

"You do? What is it?"

She bent her head and kissed him once and then

again, and then she improvised, *"Kiss your husband every day and he will want to stay and play."*

He chuckled, though there wasn't just amusement in his eyes. "I like it," he said, and with no effort at all released his arms from their restraints to wrap them around her and hold her close to him. His mouth covered hers with fire and rain, hot and pelting. With equal enthusiasm she deepened the kisses, stretching her body flat atop his, his head in her hands.

"Me too," she murmured as he rolled her under him, nibbling and kissing and licking his away along her jaw and down her neck—one big hot hand splayed lovingly over her abdomen. Her mind grew dim under the onslaught of sensations, too many coming too fast to decipher individually. The taste, the smell, the feel of him mingled with the pounding of her heart, with the shiver of her nerves and the greedy, yearning throbbing deep inside her.

She raised her head off the bed to press her lips to his neck. It felt too heavy and cumbersome for her neck to support, and she had to give up. Head back, chin in the air, she reveled in the pleasure, barely aware of the sharp edges of paper poking against her cheek—though it was vaguely distracting. Euphorically, she raised a hand, picked up the offending annoyance, and threw it in an unclear direction.

The little green book sailed through the air, its pages ruffling like leaves in the wind. It came to rest sideways against the packing boxes, open to page 64.

In finance, Chapter 11 is saved to talk about what to do when things go wrong, when plans fail, when disaster is imminent, when bankruptcy must be declared.

Here, we've saved Step 11 for the same reasons, but also to set it aside as the most important step to be learned in order to achieve your own happiness; to illustrate that all the other steps are useless and ineffective unless they are first coupled with the lesson learned in Step 11. Without it, nothing will ever be enough for you; no happiness will satisfy you; your heart will never know peace. And so . . .

STEP 11

*This above all, to thine own self be true
And it must follow
as the night the day
Thou canst not then be false to any man.*
— *William Shakespeare*

Be you. Be the best you can be. Be all that you can be. Make the most of who you are, because that's all there is of you. Listen to your heart. Be honest with yourself. Your true happiness lies within you.

THE EDITOR'S CORNER

With these, our last LOVESWEPTs, so many thanks are in order, it's impossible to know where to start. I feel a little like those people at awards ceremonies—afraid of leaving someone off the "thank you" list.

It goes without saying that we owe our biggest thanks to the authors whose creativity, talent, and dedication set LOVESWEPT apart. As readers, you've experienced firsthand the pleasure they brought through their extraordinary writing. . . . Love stories we'll never forget, by authors we'll always remember. Nine hundred and seventeen "keepers."

Our staff underwent a few changes over the years, but one thing remained the same—our commitment to the highest standards, to a tradition of innovation and quality. Thanks go out to those who had a hand in carrying on that tradition: Carolyn Nichols, Nita Taublib, Elizabeth Barrett, Beth de Guzman, Shauna Summers, Barbara Alpert, Beverly Leung, Wendy McCurdy, Cassie Goddard, Stephanie Kip, Wendy Chen, Kara Cesare, Gina Wachtel, Carrie Feron, Tom Kleh, and David Underwood.

Special thanks go to Joy Abella. Joy often said that being an editor for LOVESWEPT was her dream job and not many people got to realize their dreams. Thanks, Joy, for helping us realize how lucky we all were to have been a part of this remarkable project. ☺

Finally, thank you, the readers, for sharing your thoughts and opinions with us. Fifteen years of LOVESWEPTs was possible only because of your loyalty and faith. We hope you will continue to look for books by your favorite authors, whom you've come to know as friends, as they move on in their writing careers. I'm sure you'll agree they are destined for great things.

With warm wishes and the hope that romance will always be a part of your lives,

Susann Brailey

Susann Brailey

Senior Editor